STO
V

ALLEN COUNTY PUBLIC LIBRARY

**FRIENDS
OF ACPL**

3 1833 05799 1934

D1171308

A CRITERION BOOK

FOR YOUNG PEOPLE

WAR DOG

Henry Treece

WAR DOG

Illustrated by Roger Payne

Criterion Books • New York

Copyright © 1962 by Henry Treece

Illustrations copyright © 1962 by Brockhampton Press Ltd.

First American edition 1963

Library of Congress Catalog Card Number: 63-12461

This book was first published in Great Britain in 1962
under the same title by Brockhampton Press Ltd.

Manufactured in the United States of America

U. S. 1226860

Contents

WAR DOG

1 · Young Warriors

OF all the great war hounds of the fierce Catuvel-launi, Rhianna was the finest. Proud in her spiked bronze collar, she stood as high as a man's hip, and could drag down wolf or stag with no aid from her old master, Garroch of the Long Sword. In battle against the Iceni folk of the more northern flat-lands, she had made a great name for herself, breaking through the spearmen and, after a terrible fight, even dragging the Icenian king, Prasutagus, from his bronze-plated chariot.

When, by great good luck, Prasutagus got back to his feast hall at Venta Icenorum covered in wounds, he commanded his bard to make a song about the ferocious hound which had almost robbed him of his kingdom and his life.

Set to the harp, the song went:

> *'Rhianna! Rhianna!*
> *Great be the name of one*
> *Who grasps the iron-clad king*
> *In her white jaws,*
> *And shakes him like a child*
> *Shaking a corn-doll!*
>
> *Among the bear, the wolf;*
> *Among the lynx, the tuskéd boar,*
> *Her scent strikes terror*
> *Down the woodland glades*
> *And in the rocky dens.*
> *Lucky the folk who have such hounds!*
>
> *Fortunate the king*
> *Whose crown is guarded by*
> *Rhianna! Rhianna, of the long fangs!'*

His warriors chanted these words, rattling their swords on their shield-rims and shouting loudly whenever Rhianna's name was mentioned, as though they too were proud of her.

When old king Cymbeline of the Catuvellauni got to hear of this song, he laughed until the rafters rang and then sent for his hound-keeper, Garroch of the Long Sword, who lived in a village three miles from Camulodunum.

Garroch did not know what sort of mood the king was in, for he was wearing his blue war-paint in streaks across his broad face, and his heavy black bearskin cloak made him look hunched and enormous. So Garroch flung himself down before the king's chair and knocked his forehead on the ground in the sign of obedience.

But King Cymbeline came down the wooden steps and raised him gently. Then, smiling, he placed a bracelet of twisted dark gold about Garroch's wrist and said, 'By Mabon and all the eagles, it warms my heart to hear that your bitch Rhianna has humbled the pride of that young fool, Prasutagus! Now, perhaps, we shall have some peace along the border for a while. See to it, Garroch, that Rhianna is rewarded. Send her on no more war-forays for six months, see that she is never beaten, and take her one of my own sheep as a special prize.'

Then, as Garroch backed away from the presence of that awe-inspiring king, Cymbeline called for another cup of mead and shouted at the retreating hound-keeper, 'And do not forget to tell her that her king has sent her the sheep-meat! I do not want her to drag me from my war-chariot when next I travel among the villages!'

That was in the snow-time; by early spring, Rhianna made her master doubly proud by having a litter of puppies.

Four of them were grey and white, but the fifth and the biggest was pure black.

As this puppy first tottered about the straw-filled enclosure on his thick, furry legs, Garroch looked down

9

on him and smiled. 'Look, Gwyn,' he said to his warrior-son, 'here is a hound for you to have at last; one worthy of the horseman who rides beside the prince, Caratacus. This shall be your war dog, my son.'

Gwyn the Golden nodded and shook his corn-coloured plaits. 'At the moment he seems more concerned about his supper,' he said. 'Look how he tries to push the other dogs aside!'

Old Garroch watched and said, 'That is a good sign. He will be a real fighter, that one. What he does now, in play to his little brothers, he will do in all seriousness to the enemy, when he gets his war-teeth. He will fling them aside so that we can ride through to the attack in our chariots. What will you name him, my son?'

Gwyn the Golden thought for a while, then answered, 'He shall be called Bran, because he is as black as a crow—and because of all the dogs I have seen he is most worthy to serve the king. So it is right that he should bear the name of an ancient king himself.'

2 · The Trader

WHILE the spring-sowing was going on, a trading-ship from Sardinia came into the harbour that served Camulodunum, seeking horse-hides and hunting-dogs. The captain was a dark-skinned, hook-nosed fellow, whose oiled black hair hung in ringlets down the side of his face. He laughed rather more than was necessary and made a great show of rubbing his fat hands together whenever he was bargaining.

Most of the tribesfolk in the surrounding villages thought he was a very funny man, with his long striped robes and his red headcloth, and the boys followed him round from hut to hut, walking pompously as he did and imitating all his gestures behind his back.

Once, he caught one of the boys doing this, and would have beaten him with the long ebony staff he always carried; but, just when the stick was raised, the boy's eldest brother came from a hut, wearing the war paint and carrying a long wicker shield and a bronze-headed axe. The trader-captain suddenly began to laugh then and to tell the boy what a clever fellow he was with his imitations. He even groped in his pouch and gave the lad a little silver coin that had come from as far away as Syria.

One of the old tribesmen, sitting by the fire in the middle of the compound roasting the leg of a sheep, saw all this and said to his friend, 'Mark my words, comrade, this trader is a sly dog. I would not trust him as far as I could throw him.'

His friend, an old warrior lame in one leg, answered, 'And that would not be very far—he is so fat! I am reminded of a hog that has been out foraging too long, and has over-stuffed himself with acorns.'

The women, standing with their clay pots and goatskin bags beside the well, thought the same; and they were right.

Gwyn the Golden was away at the sowing in a big field over the far hill, pacing round the boundary of white stones and calling out the barley-blessing as the peasants scattered the grain into the shallow furrows. A chieftain always had to do this, or it was thought that the seed would not sprout. If he had been at home nothing untoward would have happened; but, as it was, the trader pushed his inquisitive way into the byre where Rhianna lay suckling her puppies, and instantly rubbed his fat hands at the sight of the brood.

'Ah, such fine hounds!' he whispered to his compan-

ion, his gold ear-rings jingling with excitement. 'I
could make a small fortune out of these little beasts in
Southern Gaul!'

One of Gwyn's herdsmen passed through, on his way
to the house to collect his food-ration for the day. He
was a careless fellow, lazy and ill-tempered, whose folk
had come from an inland tribe to join the Catuvellauni.
The trader approached him with a clever smile and said,
'Master, I am admiring these dogs. True, they are rather
small, and their coats are nothing to boast about—but,
as you may have heard, I am a generous man and, no
doubt, I could find some fool in Gaul to buy them from
me, at a small profit. What do you say, will you sell
them?'

The herdsman, who knew little about the hounds and
cared less, grunted and shrugged his shoulders. At this,
the trader slapped him on the back and called him a
wise bargainer. Then he and his companion snatched up
the puppies and tried to pull Rhianna to her feet.

Alone, she would never have gone; but when she saw
her puppies being carried away she followed, puzzled
and growling.

Gwyn strode into the village a little later to see his
stupid herdsman still muttering and gazing down at a
handful of small and almost worthless coins which the
trader had pushed into his hand.

'Why, you madman!' shouted Gwyn, when the man
had told him what had happened. 'Those dogs are worth
more than you are yourself—especially Rhianna and
Bran. If that thief of a shipman gets away to sea with

them, I will have you beaten until you howl for mercy!'

The frightened herdsman flung the coins into the dust and fell to his knees, begging his master's pardon; but Gwyn did not stop to listen to him. Instead, he leaped on to the back of a stallion that was standing outside the byre and clattered off between the huts like an avenging fury.

At first he feared that the traders had got clear away; but over the second rise towards the harbour he came upon them.

They were clustered round Rhianna, who had decided to sit down and would go no farther. She was such a strong and heavy creature that no amount of pushing or pulling would move her.

As Gwyn topped the rise, he saw the shipman strike at her with his long staff, his dark face ugly with anger. But Rhianna was no cowardly cur to be intimidated in that way; she had been trained for war and blows and had spent half her life running among the javelins.

Gwyn laughed to see her catch the ebony staff in her great jaws and snap it into two pieces. Then, while the trader was still waving his arms about and crying out that his stick had been worth a fortune, Gwyn cantered down, pushing the stallion so close to the clustered traders that they scattered in fear from the great horse.

'So, besides being a beater of little boys you are a common dog-thief!' the warrior called to the merchant, who was now almost in tears.

'It is a lie!' the man answered, his dark eyes widening as he watched Gwyn slowly drawing the long iron

14

sword from its sheath. 'I paid good money to the owner of these dogs, I swear it, before all the gods!'

Gwyn edged the stallion towards the merchant, the sunlight running up and down his long blade as he pointed it carefully at the wretch's throat.

'Do not swear to the gods, man,' he said quietly, 'but pray to them, and humbly, for in a little minute you will be explaining to them how you came to be a spirit.'

The other traders had run as far away as their breath would carry them, and were now staring back, many of them half-hoping that the stern-faced Celt on the horse *would* use his sword on their miserable bully of a master.

But, after all, he did not. He waited until the gibbering trader had worked himself into a frenzy of terror and was beating his forehead on the ground, then he gave the man a hard slap across the back with the flat of the blade, sending him spread-eagled into the dust.

'From this day onward,' he said with contempt, 'you may call at other ports as you please—but never put in here. If you do, we will set your stupid head upon our stockade to frighten the crows away from the corn; for that is all you are, at heart—a scarecrow!'

Then, gathering the whimpering puppies once more and calling gently to Rhianna, he turned and spurred his stallion back towards the village.

3 · The Hunt

AFTER the affair of the Sardinian trader, greater care
than ever was taken of Rhianna and her puppies.
Garroch set a warrior to guard them every night, for he
believed that wherever the merchant put into port, he
would spread the story of this handsome litter, and
good war dogs were so scarce among the southern tribes
at this time that others might try to do what he had
attempted.

But, luckily, no one came to steal the dogs, and so
they grew up, strong and handsome, in the months that
followed. Rhianna taught them to fight by pretending
to snap at them and then drawing away. At first, their
small milk-teeth were harmless; but as they lost these
teeth and grew more strong, their mother had to use all

her skill in avoiding them. Sometimes, if they were feeling especially frisky, the dogs would form a gang and would try to attack her in earnest.

When this happened and Rhianna was rolling from side to side in the straw, it was always the biggest puppy, Bran, who came to her rescue, as he thought. Then he would stand over his mother and give the most ferocious growl as he swung his head this way and that, driving the others back.

Gwyn loved this sight so much that he used to fetch the other warriors to watch it, until, one day, Garroch of the Long Sword said, 'Your black dog is ready to learn his trade now, my son. We must get the black-smith to make a light collar for him.'

Bran hated to leave his family, and for two whole days, after the smith had fixed the collar, he leaped about growling and rubbed against the stone wall of his pen; but the new collar would not come off.

'Wait till you get your big war collar with the spikes,' said the blacksmith to him. 'Then you'll know you are carrying some weight, Bran.'

Gwyn went into the pen and lay down with Bran on the sweet hay and held the dog's paw. Putting his face next to the dog's jaws, as a sign of trust, he whispered, 'Be a good boy, then, Bran! Be patient, lad, and you shall ride with a king one day.'

But Bran was not bothered about kings just then. He was still thinking that life had been happy when he was snuggling close to his great mother, among his merry jostling brothers, and that this collar was hard and uncomfortable. Bran did not know that the band of metal was meant to protect his throat when he came across wolves or bears in the thick oak forests that surrounded Camulodunum.

A year later Bran had forgotten that this collar existed, though; he had grown so used to it. He had grown used to his young master, Gwyn the Golden, also. In fact, as is the way with war dogs, he had now no memories at all of Rhianna—which was just as well. A war dog must be single-minded; he must adore his master above all else. And this Bran did.

Just occasionally, perhaps when he was tired out, or had been bitten by a wolf, or slashed by a wild cat, Bran half-recalled those warm snug days when he was in the straw, and other furry creatures—his brothers—rolled beside him, trying their little white teeth on his long ears, or pushing against him for milk from the patient mother. But these dreams passed and Bran soon came to learn that rough give-and-take which a war dog must know, if he is to survive.

Gwyn was kind enough, that is true; but he now had a quickly-growing hound to train, one who would soon be capable of killing an unarmed man, and he had to take no chances. So, although Bran usually fed on the best of things, such as oatmeal and sheep-meat, there were days when all war dogs must be starved, to make them keener in the chase.

At first, in his lonely enclosure, Bran hated such days and even wondered whether Gwyn had stopped loving him. He would prowl round and round the pen, howling and trying to leap the walls. But they were too high, and no one seemed to hear his howling. So, in the end, he would just sit still in the dust and wait, his tongue lolling, his mind a blank.

And then, at the dawn-time, there would be the high screaming of horns and the impatient thumping of horses' hooves. Gwyn would be at the gate, shouting and calling to Bran, 'Come out, you lazy wretch! Come with us to hunt the deer! Dare you come, Bran? Dare you?'

And young Bran would give a yelp of delight and race towards his master, hoping that Gwyn would let him leap up and lick his bearded face. But when the other men of the tribe were about, Gwyn would beat the dog down—though as gently as he dared—and call out, 'Come on, there are three roe bucks in the spinney, waiting to be killed! Run, you lazy sluggards, and a pig's death to the last one in at the kill!'

Some of the old hounds, who had accepted the collar when King Cymbeline was almost a young man, knew what these words meant. . . A pig's death was a dreadful affair of ropes and knives and squealing. The veteran hounds bayed louder and leaped higher when Gwyn spoke those words, as though they would be first in at the horn-sounding, whoever was last!

And Bran caught from them some sense of the deep seriousness of the hunting. When he was only half-grown, he went in with two veteran hounds to bring out a she-wolf that was standing guard over her litter. He saw her flaring amber eyes and the yellow fangs that she displayed towards him under her curled lip. This frightened him in a strange deep way, but Bran surged on and met her, chest to chest. The grey wolf went

20

down, slashing at him all the time; but Bran locked his jaws grimly and held on.

When the shag-haired men came through the clearing, they saw the two veteran dogs standing to one side, their tongues lolling, their thin lips slavering, just as though they were weighing up young Bran's chances of surviving that hunting season.

Gwyn ran up and put his javelin through the wolf bitch, for there was still some harm left in her. Then he picked Bran up and carried him back to the hunting-cart. The young dog was red from paw to throat, but he had not felt his wounds while the fight was on.

Afterwards, as the cart jolted back towards the village, he lay among the carcasses of deer and wild cat, and whimpered a little.

But Gwyn came to him before nightfall and washed his wounds clean, and gave him the hind-legs of a hare to eat.

Among the tribes it was forbidden for a man to kill the hare or eat it; but if the hare fell down a cliff-face and broke his own neck, that was different. Then he could be fed to the dogs, and not even the grey-bearded old Tree-priests, the Druids, in their dirty woollen robes, could argue against that.

So Bran ate the hare-meat and licked his master's hand for bringing it to him in the straw.

The young dog's next task was to face a warrior. This he did when he was less than two years old.

4 · The Testing

IT was a great day for the villagers, the tribesmen of the Catuvellauni, who were held to be among the finest warriors of Britain. 'The Testing of the Dogs', it was called; for on this day, the second day after the tribe had returned from the midsummer meeting at Stonehenge, and while thoughts of sacrifices were still in men's minds, every young war dog who came near to reaching his full growth was required to show what strength and bravery he had, against certain warriors.

This testing took place in a large round hollow that lay among the downs, three miles inland from Camulodunum. The warriors whom the dogs faced were themselves prisoners or slaves; men who might gain their release if they pleased old King Cymbeline and the folk who crowded the slopes, by their courage.

Bran was led there and placed in a large wicker pen until the cow's horn blew and it was his turn. He was very hungry and very confused in his mind by the barking and shouting that had gone on all morning, and he wondered why Gwyn had not been to see him that day.

The dog in the next pen had been whimpering all the morning, and this disturbed Bran. He barked back at the dog, telling him to be quiet and to take things as he found them.

But the dog whimpered all the more, and this angered Bran, who, by now, was becoming short-tempered. Then, when a dog-handler came and flung open the door of the wicker pen, Bran came out cautiously, looking round under the shaggy mop of hair that hung over his eyes, to see if they had brought food for him.

But there was no food : instead, a party of boys came with long sticks and pushed and poked Bran until he loped down a parting in the crowds and suddenly found himself in the bowl of the amphitheatre, facing a short dark man whose hair was secured by white bone pins.

This was Mathonwy, a Silurian from the far west, who had been captured in battle half a year before, and was famed as a swordsman among his savage people. But today he carried no sword; only a short thick stave, and a round wicker shield on his left arm.

Bran stopped a few yards from him and sniffed the air. The man was wearing a horse-hide kilt and light running-shoes of deerskin, instead of the heavy woollen cloak, tunic and breeches favoured by the men of the Catuvellauni. This puzzled Bran, and he went forward curiously to find out what sort of man this was.

Mathonwy, whose freedom depended on his showing against the hound, gave the war-cry of his own folk and ran to meet Bran, whirling his stave.

It took Bran on the shoulder and then on the flank, before he knew what was happening. As he gave ground, the crowds sitting on the slope of the hollow called out, 'So much for your war dog, Gwyn the Golden ! See, he runs from a little Silurian with a stick !'

Gwyn, who sat next to the prince, Caratacus, glowered and bit the end of his moustache.

'Wait till the fellow tries to strike again,' he said in low tones to the prince. 'Then he may wish he had more than a stick to defend himself with!'

But, in spite of these words, Gwyn was not really sure what Bran would do.

Mathonwy soon found out, for as he plunged on, meaning to rap Bran smartly on the muzzle, and put him to flight, the dog slid to one side, and, as the Silurian's hand came downwards, took him sharply by the wrist and gave a tug of his great shaggy head.

The crowd yelled as the warrior lay on the turf under the forelegs of the dog, trying frantically to get the little wicker shield over his head to protect it. The short stave had flown through the air when Bran first gripped the man's wrist, and now lay yards away and unreachable.

Caratacus turned to Gwyn with a smile and said, 'That was a clever throw, my friend. You must have been training Bran to wrestle!'

Before Gwyn could reply, the Silurian had given a great heave and had got one of his lightly-shod feet under the dog. But once again, Bran was too quick for him and, slipping away suddenly, had taken the man by the great bunch of black hair at the top of his head and was shaking him as he would have done a wild cat —or a hare, if no one was looking!

Now Mathonwy had cast aside his useless wicker shield and was doing his best to punch at the dog, but each time Bran slid away from the blows, though he never let go of the man.

In a real battle, the war dogs were trained to hold on to the enemy until their masters could run up with javelin or sword. But this was different, and, although many of the warriors in the crowds were crying out that Gwyn should go down and put an end to the Silurian, the old King Cymbeline stood up before his throne of painted wood and called out, 'Enough! Bran has proved himself already. Let no blood be shed. The Silurian shall go free, back to his own folk, now.'

As Gwyn ran down into the hollow to loosen the dog's jaws, a burly dark-jowled man in a long white cloak who sat beside the king said, in a slow foreign accent, 'The Emperor Caligula would be pleased to receive such a hound, my lord. This dog whom you call Bran would cause great amusement for the folk of Rome. We could set him against leopards, or even against young lions.'

But the prince Caratacus stared at this man in the white cloak, who wore his dark hair closely-cropped and his heavy face shaven, and said, 'Ambassador, Bran shall never go to Rome, that I promise you! Let the Emperor buy his dogs from Gaul, if he must have them. The conquered Gauls would sell their souls to please a Roman—but we are Catuvellauni, not Gauls! We are a free-folk, still!'

The Roman put on that stern expression which they were so fond of when dealing with tribesmen, but Caratacus only smiled back at him and fingered the enamelled hilt of his broad-bladed dagger, as though issuing a silent warning. King Cymbeline hid a smile behind his own heavily-ringed hand, as though he were

26

pleased with his son's proud words. Then he said, 'You have said enough, my son. If you say more, the Ambassador Gracchus will think we are barbarians—in spite of our gold coinage and the scents our ladies have brought from Alexandria!'

The Roman, put out by the words of Caratacus, gave a weary and cynical smile. He half-turned to King Cymbeline and said in a low voice, 'There are those who say that your coins are much like those that the rude peasants of Greece use, my lord. And that the scents your ladies import from Alexandria are diluted five times before the traders deliver them.'

But King Cymbeline was a merry red-faced man who thought little about Roman jibes—or about Romans themselves, indeed. He slapped the wry-faced Ambassador on the thigh and said, 'Come, man, let us have no more of this woman's bickering. It ill becomes a warrior. Let us drink to this young dog, Bran, who has today shown you what British war-hounds are capable of. A good dog is worth a good toast, so be contented!'

Bran knew nothing of this; he was happy enough to know that he sat in the wagon with Gwyn, among the hay, and that his master was fondling him and calling him by brave names. His heart was full and at that moment Bran felt he would dare to face a hundred Silurians, if Gwyn wished it. Bran could offer no more.

Perhaps both he and his master—yes, and King Cymbeline, too, for all his bluff courage—might have felt less content with the future if they had seen and heard what happened that very night, inside the house of the Roman Ambassador.

In a small room, made even more private by the heavy wall-hangings, and only dimly lit by three oil lamps of moulded bronze, Gracchus the Ambassador was talking quietly with Mathonwy the Silurian.

'You are now ready for your journey back to your own tribes in the west,' said the Roman. 'I command you to travel secretly, by night if possible, so that no one knows where you have gone. And when you reach your own king, tell him that the days of the proud Catuvellauni are numbered. Tell him that one day, before long, the Legions of Rome shall stand as masters in this land. Our Emperor, Caligula, is already massing his fighting-men and ships for that purpose. And further tell your king that if he is wise he will gather his own warriors, to strike at the men of Cymbeline from behind, while we of Rome attack from the front. Caligula will not forget you when the time comes, my friend.'

The Silurian bowed his dark head before the Roman. 'This shall be done, lord,' he said in his rough accent.

The Ambassador took up a leather bag from a marble-topped table by his side, and flung it to the Silurian. The bag jingled, as though it contained coins.

The Roman heard it and said, 'Not British rubbish, friend! This is Roman gold, with the proud face of our Emperor struck upon its side. It may be spent *anywhere in the world*. Such is the power of Rome.'

The Silurian bowed again, and went from the little room as silently as a shadow.

5 · Black News

IT was the time of the sacred fires, when the frost lay heavy and white on all the trees and fields, and old men in the villages shook their heads gravely and wondered whether there would be enough grain and meat to see the folk through the winter that lay ahead.

But in the country, five miles from Camulodunum, the prince, Caratacus, had no such misgivings.

'Hoi! Hoi!' he called, his red cloak floating behind him as he rode along the ridge, 'I scent a buck! I scent a buck! A gold collar for the first dog to drag him down, and an iron sword for the dog's master!'

Caratacus looked splendid as he rode among his two score of trusted warriors that day. On his head he wore a round bronze helmet from which stood up two great curved horns of silver. About his throat gleamed a broad collar of dark gold, inlaid with small roundels of red and blue enamels. His tunic and breeches were of the finest bleached linen, dyed in coloured squares at the edges. The red leather which was bound, criss-cross, about his strong legs had been brought by the traders from as far away as Spain. The sword which bobbed up and down on his hip as he galloped had a hilt of ivory from Libya and a pommel of bright red coral, carved delicately into the shape of an acorn. His yellow hair was braided with Egyptian silk; his fine nose jutted forth like the beak of the golden eagle. He was a prince that any warrior might be proud to follow and to die for.

By his side rode Gwyn the Golden, only a little less splendid than his prince. Bran loped proudly at the heels of Bel, Gwyn's jet-black stallion, the hound of a warrior who was the friend of a prince.

Now the hillside was covered with shouting men, neighing horses and snuffling hounds. The cold air echoed with the excited noises of the chase. It was as though half of Britain was on the move, such a thundering of hooves there was, such a deep-throated baying of dogs.

Gwyn leaned back from his high sheepskin saddle and called out, 'Hoi, Bran! Hoi! A gold collar for you before the hunt is up, my lad! See to it, Bran! See to it!'

He had scarcely shouted out these words when, at the brow of the hill, where dark pine trees stood against the grey sky, a strange figure appeared, its arms up-raised.

The prince pulled up his charging horse and pointed. 'Look, brothers,' he said, 'it is one of the Old Ones, the Tree men, who bids us halt in our hunting.'

The horsemen dragged back on the reins and beat their hounds to silence with the bull-hide whips they carried. When the Tree men spoke it was well for other men to be silent, even kings and princes.

The strange figure on the hill-top was dressed in a tattered old gown of grey wool, which flapped about his thin legs in the keen wind. His long hair and beard were

as grey and as tattered as his robe. About his head he wore a circlet of dried leaves plucked from the sacred oak.

His old voice, coming down to the hunters from the ridge, sounded as dry and crackling as the oak-leaves themselves.

'Caratacus the Prince,' he called. 'Cease your hunting. Cease this merriment, my lord. Today one has died who will put a crown of gold upon your head. And today boats have set sail that bear men who will snatch away that crown before your head has grown accustomed to its weight. Cease your sport, O King! Now there is another sort of hunting for you all, and the buck you pursue is called Aulus Plautius. He will not be an easy one to drag down, no, not with all your fine hounds, my lord!'

Caratacus clenched his fists and called out, 'Speak in plain words, man, and not in riddles. I am in no humour for riddles, I say!'

But even as the warrior spoke, the gaunt Tree man slipped into the dark shadows of the pine wood and vanished from sight.

Gwyn said, 'Shall I follow him, lord?'

But Caratacus shook his tawny head and said grimly, 'No, brother. I would not have you risk such a curse as this Druid might put upon you for disturbing him. And, in any case, his message is plain enough now that I have thought about it for a moment. It seems that my father, Cymbeline, has died in Camulodunum, and that I have been elected as King of the Catuvellauni. It seems also that the new Roman Emperor, Claudius, has set sail against us at last—after all those threats the madman Caligula kept flinging at us over the narrow sea. Aulus Plautius is the Roman general. If he is truly coming here, then we have something more than hunting to think about!'

The prince gave a wave of the hand and his hunting-party swung their ponies round to begin the ride back to their tribal citadel, Camulodunum, over the downs white with hoar-frost, and through the dense oak forests, where in the darkest depths the wild cat scuffed among the fallen leaves for whatever he could find, mouse, rat or vole; and where, far down the rides, lonely wolves howled and snuffled, scenting the distant horses and feeling the grip of the winter hunger tightening once more upon their empty bellies.

'Come, Bran,' called Gwyn to his hound. 'Do not stand all day sniffing at a quarry that is out of your reach. There will be time enough for hunting another day, if the gods wish it . . . If Mabon and Belatucader wish it. Though it runs strongly in my mind that our orders must first come from Morrigu the War God, Morrigu of the Black Ravens.'

The Prince Caratacus turned in his saddle and said grimly, 'There will also be time for talking to dogs another day, my friend! Our task now is to give my father the King a good send-off on the funeral pyre and, even while that is being done, to pass the fiery cross among the villages. We shall need every warrior we can call upon now.'

Bran heard the men talking so seriously and gazed up at them from under his shaggy mat of hair, wondering what their words meant. He had looked forward to the fierce hunting—and yet now everyone was turning back. There was no more shouting, no more howling of horns—only silence. This puzzled Bran.

6 · *The Storm Breaks*

IN the great square of Camulodunum, where the
houses, pillared after the Roman manner but made of
wood, rose high above men's heads, stood the funeral
pyre of the dead king, Cymbeline. It was of oak and
ash and beech, piled in faggots to the height of two tall
men. At its summit the dead king, dressed in his finest
body-armour, sat, propped in his war-chariot, his two
javelins pointing to the dark sky. At his feet lay three
of his most famous hounds, dead like their master. Before the chariot his two black stallions, in all their
trappings and plate-gold, were stretched out on their
sides, ready to gallop away to the Isle of the Blessed
after the roaring flames had licked about them and had
set them free from their bodies.

Bran, in the foremost rank of the warriors and chief-
tains, watched Druids sprinkle the wood with the
sacred libations of milk, honey and bull's blood. And
then the torches were flung upon the pyre. A wild wind
from the sea fanned the flames until they seemed to
gobble up the wood as a greedy man tears a chicken
with his teeth. Bran watched the war-chariot begin to
blaze and then, for one terrifying moment, it seemed
about to topple off its pinnacle and crash among the
grey-robed priests. If Gwyn had not held him close and

U! S. 1226860

whispered to him, he would have turned round and run for his life back to his wicker pen behind the houses.

But the threatened disaster was forgotten as the chariot sank deeper into the heart of the fire.

Then Caratacus, who had been the prince and who was now the King, raised his hands above his tawny head and cried out, 'Fair journey, my father. May your horses run swiftly and your hounds stand guard over you. May the javelins in your hand never swerve from their target. The praise of your people, the Catuvellauni, go with you. Farewell, and speed to your chariot wheels!'

Then the women of the place fell upon their knees and covered their heads with their cloaks and shawls as a sign of reverence. But the men clashed their long swords of iron or bronze upon the rims of their round shields and echoed the words of Caratacus: 'Speed to your chariot wheels!'

As the last ashes of the chariot crumbled and fell down among the blazing embers, a man cantered into the square on a shaggy hill-pony, his right arm dangling and useless, a bandage of dirty linen about his head. He sat swaying in the saddle for a while and then, sighting Caratacus, cried out in a voice heavy with weariness, 'My great lord, from the tokens I carry on my body you will know that it is time to leave the funeral pyre. *They* have landed, the men of Rome. We held them as long as we could at the marshes, but they are fearless, and as many as the ants in summer.'

Caratacus the King turned and called out, 'Where are we to meet them, fellow?'

The man sank down on his pony's neck with tiredness. His eyes were rimmed with red; his face was deathly white. But still he smiled—the strange smile of one who has lived through too much death and destruction.

'Great one,' he whispered, 'it is not our task to meet them. They are already coming here. *They will meet us*—and when we clash together, may the dead King upon the pyre look down and give us his aid, for we shall need it!' The last words were barely out before he fell from his pony.

Out from the crowd ran a strange and shambling figure, a man no taller than a boy, but as broad in the shoulder as a door of the King's barn. He was dressed in a long garment of patchwork cloth of many colours, but now faded by sun and rain. On his grotesque and wrinkled brown head, he wore a high conical cap of catskin, with the tails dangling down on either side, mingling with his long and uncombed black hair. In his hands he carried two broad laths, shaped like swords, which he clashed together as he circled in his bearlike dance.

The crowd called out at the appearance of this man, 'Here comes Black Boru! Boru the Irishman, the bringer of victory! Sing to us, Boru, and let us hear if your voice has lost its sweetness!'

So, as the funeral pyre still crackled and the war dogs whined, sensing excitement in the air, Boru ran out into an open space, the children dragging at the hem of his ragged gown and, after nodding his head up and down in time to his prancing, like a war horse with

36

the smell of battle in his nostrils, clapped his hands to a broken rhythm and began to chant:

> *'I see the men in iron,*
> *Crushing the corn-shoots*
> *With their feet;*
> *Striking the apples from the boughs*
> *With javelins;*
> *Shouting, among the trumpets,*
> "Ave! Ave! Caesar!" '

Caratacus called out from his place by the dying embers, 'That goes well enough, Black Boru, but tell us the end of the tale! Let my people hear what else lies in wait for them? Speak without fear, old fellow!'

The Irishman stopped in his clashing of the wooden swords and made the pretence of wiping tears from his eyes. Then, in a high and wailing voice, such as women put on when they are mourning the dead, he sang:

> *'Oh, where are they now,*
> *The Tribunes, the Centurions?*
> *Where are they now, my friends?*
> *Ask the sly wolves who pick*
> *At the white bone in the dim wood;*
> *Ask the cautious spider*
> *Who weaves her web over the empty sockets,*
> *Deep in the hidden hollows,*
> *The hollows where the iron men*
> *Crept to be safe, but found no peace*
> *Away from the lances of the warriors!'*

As he came to the end of the chant, the young braves of the Catuvellauni rattled their spears against their hide shields and began to nod their plaited heads, like stallions working themselves into the rhythm of the charge.

Bran felt it all, deep in his heart, and tugged at the thick hide thong that kept him tied to Gwyn's wrist.

'Steady, boy, steady,' whispered Gwyn, his own lean face working with the mounting thrill of war. 'There will be time, my beauty! There will be time!'

Later that day, in the rush-lit feast-hall, the bards sang to flute and the small harp, and the mead-jar passed back and forth along the broad oak board. The fighting-men, their foreheads and chests streaked with the blue war-paint from the woad plant, ate ravenously at their meat and thumped on the table with the bone hafts of their knives. At the head of the board, high on his carved oak chair, his fur robes about his shoulders, the new King, Caratacus, smiled down on his people and said, 'My brothers, the gods are good to us in sending us such a chance to show the proud Roman of what metal we are cast. For many of us, this will be our last supper together—but who of the Catuvellauni will regret such a parting? Not I, I swear, my brothers. Not I. We are men, my brothers, and for men there is no skulking in caves while the enemy rides by. That is well enough for tender women and girls, for milch-kine and lambs. But the gods have given men a task, as they have given a task to war dogs and stallions and the wide-horned bulls. That task is to strike terror in all who come against them!'

He rose, a little unsteadily now, and held up his great curved horn-cup, rimmed with silver. 'Death to all Romans!' he shouted.

The blue-streaked tribesmen snatched up their own wine-cups and rose at the tables. Their hair was flung back like the manes of horses, their wide eyes glistened in the flickering light of the wall-torches.

'Death to all Romans!' they called.

The stallions, tethered to their mangers at the far end of the feast-hall, stamped their hooves and snorted, as though they, too, answered the King's call. The war dogs jostled among the trestles in the straw and flung their great heads from side to side, sniffing and growling.

Of them all, Bran now growled the fiercest.

7 · The Battle for Camulodunum

THE day dawned bright and clear; frost stood like sprinkled silver on all the hawthorns and gorsebushes that grew on the downs a league from the city of Caratacus. Here would be held the great battle that would decide whether the Catuvellauni or the legionaries of the Emperor Claudius were to be the masters in southern Britain.

The King, Caratacus, erect in his light bronze-plated chariot, held the centre of the ridge that looked down upon the distant town. His golden hair was drawn back and bound tightly in spirals of copper so that it might not blow into his eyes. The curved bull's horns of his helmet glinted in the early sun; his blood-red cloak hung about his great frame like the curtains that cover a sacred shrine. The sheen on his broad sword-blade was seen by men half a mile away, so polished had the armourers made it during that night of preparation.

Beside him, in the chariot, stood Gwyn the Golden, leaning on his javelin, smiling as though this day was a festival when all men should be merry.

Bran, who was tethered for the time being to the axle of the chariot, gazed up at his master, adoring him, waiting for his word. Never had dog so loved a warrior;

never had warrior so fine a hound to go with him among
the falling swords and the thundering hooves.

Bran glanced back at the black stallion, Bel, who was
tied to the tail of the chariot, so that when the time
came Gwyn could leap on to his back and pursue the
flying enemy.

In the dog's heart there was a glow of pleasure that
he and Bel should be with Gwyn and the King at this

time. Black Bel sensed this, too, in the way that horses know what their masters are about. Such creatures do not need words to speak with; they have eyes to see, and hearts to understand. They have lived with men since the earliest dawn of history, and they know their masters' minds by instinct, without needing to be told.

The bowman who stood on the shaft that ran between the King's chariot-horses looked back at the warriors who stood behind him and, addressing his King in the familiar way that was the right of all Celtic freemen, said, 'It's a chill morning, Caratacus, but before the day is out we'll have these Romans sweating! When Bran and Bel get on their heels, they'll cry for mercy, I promise you!'

Caratacus the King smiled back from under his great helmet and said, 'The Gauls, who brag that they can hold up the sky on the points of their lances, are not the only men who can boast, it seems! Yet I hope that your words are true, Bedwyr. It is high time that this world saw a Roman on his knees, begging for mercy!'

Behind the ridge, a party of Trinovantes, whose chief owed allegiance to Caratacus, were circling about their charred totem pole, the hawks' feathers bobbing in their dark hair, their small round wicker shields swinging about their heads as they moved in and out of the pattern of their war-dance.

Gwyn the Golden looked back and smiled. 'They are a merry folk, these Trinovantes,' he said to his King. 'I shall watch carefully the steps of their dance when they run up against the Roman shield-wall.'

Caratacus said softly, 'I have put them behind the

chariots for a good reason, my brother. Besides, their chief owes me a tribute of fifty oxen and I want him to come whole out of this affair so that I can collect the debt!'

Then suddenly the rooks rose in black clouds from the woods below the ridge, filling the cold air with their cries of alarm. Gwyn glanced at his master and saw that the King's lips were set in a tight smile. It was then that the crowded tribesmen on the hill first heard the high skirling of the Roman war trumpets—that sound which had struck terror into the men of the sandy wastes of Africa and the ice-locked plains of Scythia.

Bran, waiting by the axle-tree, felt the hackles of his neck rise. Bel stopped pawing the ground and shuddered; the cold light flickered along the silk of his flanks and his great nostrils flared wide for an instant as he snuffed the air.

The Trinovantes halted like frozen men in their wild dancing and flung back their dark heads, eyes closed, as though speaking a last silent prayer.

A shiver passed along the high ridge as the first standard-bearers of the Romans broke cover and came into view, three hundred paces below the waiting tribesmen. The sunlight glinted on the row of golden Eagles, held proudly aloft, their medallions swinging in the breeze that swept along the shallow valley.

Gwyn counted the standard-bearers in their spotted leopard-skins . . . 'Five, ten, twenty . . . By Mabon, my King, they must have come with ten Legions,' he whispered, aghast. 'Beyond that wood must lie more warriors than we have in the whole of Britain.'

The King Caratacus nodded his great head and flung back the fold of his cloak, to free his right arm.

'They make a brave show,' he said quietly, 'but half of them are Gauls, or Africans, or Spaniards. I have met their sort before, when I travelled through Germania. They are brave enough when the going is good; but watch them when the Eagles begin to tumble! Then they fling down their swords and run into holes in the ground!'

Gwyn did not answer this. He was thinking that the Trinovantes, and even the Atrebates who had come to join them, might race these Africans to gain the nearest hole in the ground—or the closest tree for that matter. . . . But he did not say what was in his mind. The King was in no mood to listen to more words. So, instead, Gwyn busied himself in loosening Bran's hide-thong, and in whispering to the trembling hound: 'Strike sure, Bran, my darling, and don't let the horns frighten you. We have horns, too, my pretty, and ours are every bit as fearsome as those down there in the valley. Keep with the chariot, Bran, my love; and wait patiently for me in the shades if this day is unlucky for you.'

Then, along the ridge, the bull-roarers of the Catuvellauni began to buzz like angry bees, and the great hide drums started their deep-throated bellowing. Above these sounds rose the high screaming of the horns that always gave the final signal for the charge. Here and there along the hill, men suddenly lost their wits and began to tear off their body-armour, so as to run naked at the enemy. This was something that no King could stop. It went in tribes and families, this tearing-off of

44

the war-shirt; and always there were men who counted themselves braver than their fellows because of the number of scars they could display on their bodies.

Caratacus muttered, 'Poor devils! No wonder the Romans call us barbarians!'

Gwyn said quietly, 'They will have less of a load to carry to the Isle of the Blessed. This body armour is a cumbersome thing, Caratacus!'

The King was about to make some reply to this, when the first hail of arrows came up the hill, almost darkening the sky for an instant as they whirred overhead.

'Those are Scythian archers,' said the man on the chariot-shaft. 'No Roman bow can carry so far. Those are the little horn-bows from the East.'

Then Caratacus the King gave the hand-sign and the long line of chariots began to roll.

Bran gave a high yelp and strained at the leash, almost throttling himself to get down at these men whose scent was so different from that of the men he had always lived with.

8 · Strange Cavalry

THAT first shock of meeting between the Catuvellauni and the Roman shield wall was such that no
man who came out of it ever forgot it, in dream or in
waking.

The war dogs outstripped both chariots and foot-
soldiers, in a long, wavering, yelping, line. Before them,
their iron-clad prey . . . But between them and the
Romans now lay an obstacle they had not expected.
Each soldier of the Legions had flung down before him
a small hawthorn bush, so that there was a rough hedge
of boughs and cruel spines for the animals to surmount.
Even as they struggled, trying to disentangle themselves before hurling their shaggy bodies at the wall of
locked Roman shields, javelins whistled through the

46

cold air and took their toll. Bran, biting away at a branch which obstructed him, felt the pilum-point sear across his shoulder. This made him all the more angry —especially when he saw, to left and to right, that hounds he had run with in the hunts lay transfixed and writhing on the hard ground.

He broke free and hurtled at the Roman shield wall. Even as he leaped, he scented a strange scent behind those shields, behind the stern-faced men who held them so firmly against this onslaught. A scent he could not put a name to, but which struck a sort of deep terror into his heart.

Clawing and snapping savagely, he fell back from the shields, battered by spear-butts, cut by whirring sword-edges.

And even as he crouched for the next leap, the chariots came in, with a thundering of hooves and the high whinnying of horses.

Like a well-greased wheel, the Roman shields lowered for an instant, and Bran saw that behind each hard-faced legionary stood a smaller brown-faced man with a bow. Arrows hissed in the air; horses screamed, flailed with their iron-shod hooves, then tumbled this way and that, overturning their chariots, toppling the men who had ridden behind them.

Then the Roman shield wall locked again and stood firm. Above the great dark wood, ravens rose crying, scenting the kill. Bran glanced uncertainly behind him for a moment, then plunged at the shields once more. Sometimes his sharp fangs glanced off an arm-guard, sometimes a thigh-greave; but not once did he find anything which he could grip and hold on to as he had been trained.

Then a blow beside the head sent him staggering back. An arrow stuck in the ground not a finger's width from his paws.

Somewhere behind him, from among the tumbled chariots of the Catuvellauni, a voice he knew, Gwyn's voice, called out, 'Back, Bran, back!'

But the dog was dazed now and did not know in which direction to run.

It was while he half-sat, half-lay, panting and distressed, that the Roman shield wall seemed to fold away and vanish. The splendidly disciplined Legions had swung aside like great gates, to allow free passage to something else . . . But to what? Bran wondered.

He was not left wondering long, for suddenly there came a great trampling of brushwood, a high trumpeting, and that curious scent again . . .

Tall, ponderous, great creatures moved out of the wood towards the surprised Catuvellauni, their sides plated with iron, their broad foreheads painted with the sign of the golden Eagle of the Legions, ring after ring of spiked iron about their swinging trunks.

The elephant cavalry of Claudius!

On each creature's neck sat a dark-skinned man, wearing little but head-cloth and a short tunic. Bran saw the brown legs dangling and leaped to snatch at one; but the man beat him down with a short bar of pointed metal, and the dog fell back, stunned, scarcely avoiding the immense feet that shook the ground beside him.

When his senses cleared, Bran swung round, looking for his master. He saw Gwyn alone on the piled wreckage of the chariot, swinging his long iron sword and shouting.

'Up Caratacus! Up the Catuvellauni!' he yelled for all to hear.

Bran knew that war-cry as well as he knew his own name. He gave a yelp and swung round to run to where his master was needing him. Men with long Roman shields were pressing round now, thrusting up again and again with their cruel javelins. Gwyn had lost his fine helmet and his golden hair streamed in the wind. In Bran's eyes he was the finest warrior in the world.

But even a great warrior cannot stand long against ten determined Romans with shield and spear. As the war dog raced, leaping over still bodies, over the shattered remains of chariots, between the threshing hooves of horses in their last agony, he saw Gwyn go down, his long sword swinging to the end.

Then the dog's eyes clouded and his mind went blank. He knew only that he must reach Gwyn, reach him and lie on him, covering his master with his own shaggy body.

Men in plumed Roman helmets struck at him as he passed, with sword or mace, but luck was with him and they all missed.

And at last he was climbing over the body of poor Bel, the black stallion, who now lay as still as stone, then over the splintered woodwork of Gwyn's chariot.

His master lay on the floor of the chariot, his arms flung wide, his hands empty of weapons, his mouth open but silent now, his glorious hair spread about him like the glow of the summer sun. The scent that came from his dear body was quickly growing cold.

With a deep low growl of utter misery, the dog flung himself across Gwyn's sprawled body, and lay there, covering him, his shaggy head against his dead master's cheek.

For Bran, the battle was over, whoever had lost or won.

He lay there for a countless age, while the ravens rustled the cold air with their black wings, and the elephants still trumpeted in the distance.

Then a broad-shouldered man wearing the leopard-skin of a Roman standard-bearer gazed over the broken rail of the chariot. His short beard was grizzled and curly. There was little mercy in his light grey eyes.

He said to a tall shield-man beside him, 'These British dogs are useless without their masters. Here is no loot!'

Bran gazed up at him helplessly as the man in the leopard-skin brought down the butt of his great Eagle standard.

Then there was only silence, and blackness. Not even sorrow any more.

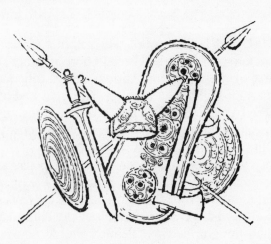

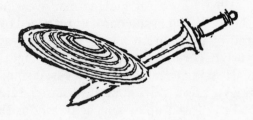

9 · The Gauls

DUSK had begun to fall when Bran's senses came
back to him. Fires had been lit here and there along
the edge of the wood, and strange voices called out to
each other, laughing and joking. The frost had broken
after the battle and now a fine drizzle fell through the
air, causing what leaves there were to whisper mysteri-
ously in the closing night.

Skin wind-breaks had been set up on poles, and in
the shelter of one of these, around a fire made of
splintered wood from the once-glorious chariots, sat a
group of hard-faced soldiers, men of the Ninth Legion,
who had flung aside their helmets and loosened their
corselets. Now they were passing the wine-skin round
in the rain, and singing, their faces wet and shining in

the firelight. A Decurion, his right arm bound in a bloody bandage, was standing over them and beating time with the broken shaft of a javelin:

'When we marched out from Tarraco,
The new swords in our hands,
The fine Centurion, he said
We'd kiss a thousand girls!

But all we've kissed is northern snow,
Or lain in southern sands;
The lads we marched with first are dead
After a thousand miles!

When I get home to Tarraco,
The devil take the army!
I'll get myself a little farm
Before they drive me barmy

With this parade, and that parade,
And "Stand up straight, my man!"
Give me a bench beneath the shade
And a wife to fill my can!

I do not ask for medals,
I do not ask for gold;
But I'd like a little rest, my boys,
Before I grow too old!

Let Caesar keep his kingdoms,
Plautius the laurel wreath;
I only pine for a quart of wine
And a stool beside the hearth!'

Bran heard them singing the jaunty little rhythms in their rough Spanish voices, voices that seemed to march together over hard roads, in time; the voices of soldiers who had stood side by side half-way across the world for twenty years. This was not like the slow wild wailing of his own folk, when the sad harp strummed in the shadows of the feast-hall.

Bran wondered what he should do. Gwyn lay stiff now beneath him and there was a vast emptiness in the dog's heart. Bel lay, a few paces away, stripped of all his battle finery, the bronze nose-guard, the golden chest-plate—even the four iron battle-shoes. The pillagers who always followed in the wake of a victorious Roman army had been at work, it seemed.

Suddenly the dog was aware that men were standing about him, one of them, a squat fellow with shaggy red hair, holding a resinous torch above him so that he could see the dog.

'Hey, hey, my comrades,' he was calling, 'this beast isn't dead after all! In spite of all his cuts and slashes, there's still a bit of life left in him! And look at that fine bronze collar he's wearing, tucked under his shaggy hair! That would melt down and make a good dagger, wouldn't it, Gretorix?'

A ragged man with a black patch over one of his eyes stepped forward and tugged back Bran's neck-hair to see the collar.

'Aye, that it would,' he said. 'Let's drag the beast back to the shelter. We can get the collar off there. You know what these Romans are if they see us looting the conquered!'

The red-haired man nodded. 'True,' he said in his guttural tones. 'If they do it, it's all right; but if we poor Gauls do it, then it's twenty lashes after morning parade and no questions asked! Who'd march with the Legions, I want to know!'

These men were Auxiliaries, helpers, and not real Roman legionaries. As they hauled Bran on to the small forage-cart which they pushed, the dog got the scent of them. They were Gauls—of that he was sure. He had smelled Gauls before, when they had come to the market at Camulodunum in the time of Cymbeline, to trade their rough red wine for oysters and horse-hides. Bran had heard his dead master, Gwyn the Golden, speak of them as rogues and traitors. The dog had not understood the words Gwyn had used—but there was no mistaking the tone of his voice when he spoke of them.

Later, when the drizzle turned to a heavy rain, the Gauls knocked out the rivets of Bran's neck-ring, and then took shears and clipped all his long hair from him, leaving him cold and desolate. They wasted nothing, the Gauls!

Bran lay, shivering and beaten, all that night in the rain, too weak to drag himself into the meagre shelter of the wood.

At some time after dawn a Roman sentry, patrolling that stretch, stopped for a while, and gazed down at him.

'So, you were a war dog,' he said softly. 'I can see that by the marks your collar left as well as by the wounds you've taken, poor fellow. Perhaps it would be a kindness to put my javelin through you. I wonder . . .'

He paused a moment, and even half-raised his spear. But just then Bran opened his eyes and looked up at the soldier. The man lowered his weapon and shook his head sadly. 'No,' he said, 'I'll not kill a fellow-warrior when he lies helpless on the ground. Here, boy, see if you can eat this!'

From the leather pouch at his side, he took a piece of black barley bread and a sliver of goat's milk cheese. Then, laying down his shield and spear, he kneeled and held the food to Bran's mouth. At first the dog did not wish to eat; but soon a ravening hunger, stronger even than his misery, came over him, and he chewed painfully at the morsels the Roman offered him.

The man smiled and nodded. 'That's a true soldier,' he said. 'A man must eat, come what may, eh, war dog? If you're here when I pass on the night watch, I'll bring you something a bit more tasty, comrade.'

Then he marched on, and Bran watched him go, almost sorrowfully.

But the dog was not there, at the wood's edge, near Camulodunum, when the good soldier went looking for him once again. Bran was three miles away from the battlefield, dragged by the merciless Gauls to the very village where he had spent his puppyhood.

But nothing was the same now; even the scents in the wet air were different. Bran smelled charred wood and the droppings of the elephants. These odours were mingled with one more terrible, which struck the dog in the face like a harsh blow: the scent of the unburied dead.

Once the party of foraging Gauls passed the place where Rhianna had first suckled Bran. The dog tottered forward, as eagerly as he could on his weakened legs; but the wattle hut was now only a heap of black rubbish. As he stood, swaying and gazing about him, bewildered, something stirred in the wreckage. It was an old woman, Old Morag, who had often fed Bran with

barley bread soaked in good cow's milk, before his teeth were strong enough to tackle bones and meat.

Her face was gaunt and black with soot. Her grey hair, unbound, hung about her shoulders like dirty rags. For a moment she rose upon her elbow and stared with wide dark eyes at the war dog.

'Dear Bran,' she said, 'have you come to this, too?'

She made a great effort and held out her thin hand towards him. The dog lurched forward, wanting to lick that old hand. But Gandoc, the man who had first found Bran among the chariots, beat the dog back with the butt of his horse-whip, shouting at him to learn his manners now that he had come among Romans. Then Gretorix, the red-haired one, went forward to the woman with a threatening club in his hand. She spoke no more to Bran, and the dog was dragged away.

Always it was the same; always beating and harsh words and scrabbling among the burned huts to find food or trinkets. The Gaulish Auxiliaries hated both the Catuvellauni and their own Roman masters—but they lost no chance of making what profit they could from this defeat at Camulodunum. Gradually their forage-carts became laden with loot—weapons, shields, helmets, cooking-pots, sacks of grain, even those greasy old sheepskins that the Catuvellauni had used as floor-coverings in the wattle huts. Once when they halted, Bran leaned against the side of the cart and suddenly scented something he knew well. It was the neck-ring of his mother, Rhianna. He gave a low whimper and tried to climb up into the cart to find the ring.

But a young boy, the son of Gandoc, beat him on the

paws with a short staff and made him get down again.

Those days were a terrible nightmare to the war dog. Often, as they travelled in the wake of the Legions, Bran wanted to attack these men who kept him prisoner, tied with a hide thong to the tail of the cart; but he was still very weak and could scarcely walk. They beat him if he even so much as bared his teeth at them, and then kept back from him what little food they usually flung down at him.

Gradually, as the party entered the great oak forests that lay along the upper reaches of the Tamesa, the dog gave up trying to fight back, and sank into a state of hopeless sullen despair. And always, wherever the Legions had been, there were burned huts and heaps of ragged bodies.

To Bran it was as though the world had suddenly ended and he was journeying through a long dark tunnel of despair.

Once Gretorix rolled him over with his foot and said with a harsh laugh to Gandoc, 'This British beast does not seem to thrive on the good food we give him. His bones show through his dirty hide, and his wounds do not seem to heal. If he looks no better by tomorrow, I will put a javelin into him. We cannot waste precious food on such a spiritless creature.'

There was much in what this man said that reached the dog's understanding. Always, from the man Gretorix, Bran had scented danger; and now that scent was stronger than ever.

That night, as soon as the men had rolled themselves in their blankets about the fires, Bran began to gnaw at the hide thong which kept him a prisoner. He could not bring much strength to the task, but the fear of Gretorix drove him on and on, and well before dawn the thong parted, to let him go free.

His heart thudding, Bran crawled past the shaggy men who sat on guard at the edge of the wood, and slipped as silently as he could among the dark bushes. No one had seen him go, and for the moment he was free again. But free for what? The dark forest that lay before him was strange and menacing. Bran had never before gone into such a place alone—Gwyn and the other warriors with their hounds had always been somewhere behind him.

But now he was alone, and too weak to defend himself.

Towards dawn, wet through and sore-footed, Bran paused by a hawthorn brake below a moss-covered heap of sandstone rocks.

Here he saw a hole, the entrance to a small cave of sorts; and from this hole came warmth. The dog, dazed with fatigue, thought of it for a moment, and then crept into the sheltering darkness.

10 · A Fish and the Tribune

FOR a moment Bran could see little in that dim cave,
apart from a mound of dried grass and bracken.
He staggered towards it and lay down, shivering. Then,
as sudden as a blow, a heavy musk-like scent came to his
nostrils. This was something he did not recognize, yet
which caused in him an abrupt fluttering of the heart,
and a strange nameless fear that seemed as old as the
earth itself.

As the dog shifted his weight in the bracken, he heard
a grunt and a deep-chested snuffling behind him. The
mound of dried vegetation quivered and then was still
once more.

It was at that moment that Bran knew the origins of
the musky smell, and of the fear that beat in his heart.
This was the winter quarters of a forest bear, and his
own stumbling entry into the cave had half-awakened
the fierce creature in its hibernation.

Bran knew well enough what strength would lie in
those great furry arms, what cruelty in those long and
slashing claws. It was one thing to face a bear in the
open, with the other hounds and the yelling javelin-
men to help; but it was another to lie, wounded, in the
enclosed space of a cave, beside such a monster—without a neck-ring or even a shaggy coat to provide pro-
tection from the fangs and deadly claws.

Now the heap of bracken began to move once again, and the bear's grunts turned to a prolonged and angry growling. It was as though the sleeping animal had caught a whiff of the dog's scent and was coming out of his deep sleep to drive away this intruder on his privacy.

Bran knew now that his hope of shelter in this warm cavern was nothing but a dream. As gently as he could, the hound began to draw himself towards the hole by which he had entered. But suddenly, behind him, the bear gave a great snort and sat up. Bran whirled about and rolled to one side as a paw struck heavily into the bracken where his head had been but a moment before. Bran bared his own fangs and struck at the paw, but it was as firm as oak. He felt himself being flung to one side, as helpless as a puppy. As he struck the rocky wall of the cave, his ears caught the sound of dry bracken rustling violently.

Never in his short life had Bran turned tail from an enemy, but now his great heart suddenly knew fear and utter humility. He rushed headlong towards the entrance hole, smelling the bear coming nearer and nearer, hurting himself as he scraped against the sharp stones to avoid those swift and deadly claws.

Before the dog had gained the entrance, a great paw came down upon his left shoulder and Bran knew from the sudden harsh agony that he had taken another wound that he could ill afford. Yet he slashed back with his own white fangs, and felt an instant of satisfaction as they plunged into that offending paw. He heard the bear give a quick gasp and a grunt of angry surprise.

Then Bran was outside, the blood coursing down his body, his jaws open as though he wanted to yell out in pain . . .

But he went silently among the undergrowth, his training as a war dog overcoming his natural instincts. He went like a crippled thing, staggering this way and that, helplessly; his only desire now being to get away from that hulking dark shape in the cave.

The bear let him go, and sank down among the bracken once more to lick his own wound and to wonder why his sleep should have been disturbed so rudely.

Bran got as far as his strength would let him before stopping. He dragged himself into a shallow hole, where the brambles came down and overhung it with their spikes; and there he lay whimpering at last.

When he became aware of things again, there had been a heavy frost, and the bramble-shoots hung like white snakes about his little lair.

His wounds had stiffened and he found that he could hardly stand.

Yet soon there came to his ears a sound which told him that he must stand—must stand, or die where he lay.

What his still keen ears had picked up was the howling of a wolf pack in the full flush of the hunt. His weary brain told him with a cruel clarity that he was now the hunted, that the wolves had picked up his scent outside the bear's cavern, and were now hot upon his trail.

Bran got to his feet somehow just as the first wolf

appeared, at the end of the long forest ride. Behind this leader loped at least six more wolves, and all moving with an intensity that warned Bran he might expect no mercy.

The dog lurched from behind the trailing white brambles and made for a dark tunnel than ran beneath a hawthorn brake. Here he might stave them off for a little while, for in that tunnel not more than one wolf could come at him at a time.

Moving on his belly, the thorns above him ripping at his tender wounds, the dog scrabbled on the chill earth, dragging himself as far from his pursuers as he was able.

But he was sick, and they were strong and hardy. Soon their young leader was snuffing at the dog's heels, little more than five paces from him.

Bran turned with a great effort and bared his teeth at the wolf. It stopped and glanced round, as though to see whether its fellows had caught up.

Then Bran turned again and crawled on, no longer able to spare the strength that would let him show even a token resistance to the pack-leader.

It was at this moment that Bran's last shred of luck ran out. The tunnel ended, the hawthorn bushes grew only sparsely now—and the first wolf saw his chance and leaped.

As the exhausted hound rolled over with the impact, his legs flailing weakly, his jaws snapping at the empty air, the other wolves ran in, their eyes flaming, their red tongues lolling.

For a time, so great was the clustering about Bran

that the wolves tore at each other in their haste to kill the dog. That was his salvation. Once or twice Bran grabbed at the muscular throat above him and heard the wolf-leader howl. Then the dog's whole world became a red riot of yelping, snuffling, slavering darkness. Bran knew vaguely that they were all tumbling this way and then that, but he had lost all sense of direction.

He had come to the point when silent death seemed preferable to him than this unending struggle of fang and claw. Gasping and shuddering for breath, he broke free for one moment, and even stood upright to bay out his last defiance, when the ground fell away from him and he felt himself plunging down and down into the darkness.

He struck the ground with a thud which drove the wind from his lungs. He was dimly aware of a stabbing pain in his right hind-leg. And then the struggle was over, and the wolves were not tearing at him any longer.

All was silent for a while, and Bran felt strangely peaceful. What he did not know was that he was dying. If he had known, it would have made no difference; there was nothing he could do to fend off the last enemy.

For an hour the wolves leaned over the rim of the bear-pit into which the dog had fallen, and scented the blood which ran from the gaping wound in his leg where the wooden stake had pierced him in his fall. Then at last, tired of slavering over a prey that would not be theirs, they swung about and ran howling once more into the forest, to seek a new quarry.

The cold night came down over the pit and, numbed by the frost, Bran's wounds ceased to trouble him. In a strange way, he even began to feel warm, as though he was lying once more on the hearth-stone in Gwyn the Golden's house. He turned his head weakly to see where Gwyn was, to see whether he was taking his supper at the long table and perhaps holding out a piece of meat on the end of his long knife, as he often did . . .

The wooden stake nearest Bran's head seemed like the blade of Gwyn's knife, but there was no meat on it. Bran reached out slowly and took the point of the stake between his teeth, to make sure. No, it was hard and cold, and there was no meat.

Then the dog began to whimper a little, thinking that his master had forgotten him. And so he fell into a strange twilight sleep, in which he saw Caratacus the King standing proudly in his war-chariot, the banner of the red dragon floating behind him, the horns of his helmet gleaming in the dying sun.

'Come, Bran!' the King was calling on the night wind. 'Come, Bran! Good lad! Good lad!'

And when that dream faded the voice still went on, though now its tones were different—it was another voice, but it spoke the same words, 'Good lad! Good lad!'

The dog was dimly conscious of a new scent which seemed to float somewhere above him. It was the scent of food, of something which Bran remembered as distantly as he remembered the sunlit days of his puppyhood. He moved his head so slightly, dilating his nostrils to take in this smell. It was only a small move-

ment and his eyes were still closed, but it was observed above.

A voice said, 'Dangle the fish a little lower, man. I saw his nostrils move then. I hope to Mithras that the hound is not past saving. He has been a brave fellow in

his time, by the looks of him; and every brave fighting-man, Roman or British, two-legged or four-legged, has a right to expect mercy after a hard battle. Mercy and justice, above all things, I say!'

Bran found the strength to open his eyes a little way as the fish, on the end of a flax-string, touched his nose. But it was not the food that interested him, he was beyond any thought of hunger; it was the voice. Momentarily, he dreamed that it was Gwyn's voice; but when his eyes could focus on the two men who leaned over the edge of the bear-pit, he saw that neither of them was Gwyn.

One was a shaven-headed Roman legionary, with a long iron shield strapped to his back, and wearing a thick leather jerkin. The other was younger and more splendid; the blue cloak of a cavalry leader hung from his broad shoulders, the tall scarlet plume of a Tribune stood up from the polished bronze helmet on his handsome head.

As Bran gazed wearily upwards, the Tribune called down to him in a gentle voice, 'Have courage, comrade! We'd not let a warrior die in a ditch, my friend, if we could help it. Titus the Decurion shall come down and bring you up, and then we'll take you to my tent.'

Bran sighed and closed his eyes again. And presently he felt himself being lifted gently from the sharpened stake that had wounded him. The Decurion with the dark, shaven head was a strong man—but his hands were as kind as those of a woman. Bran tried to lick them, but the effort was too much for him, and he sank back, a dead weight now, as the Decurion placed him tenderly in the arms of the splendid Tribune.

11 · A New Master

FOR many days Bran lay between life and death, sometimes scarcely breathing. Klymenes, the Alexandrian physician, a dark-skinned man with an oiled and curled black beard, bent over him, administering potions and salves, and seeing to it that Bran was kept warm and clean.

Often the hard-faced Decurion and his men would look in to see how the war dog was progressing, and gradually their stern faces began to take on a happier expression as they stooped and patted him with hands more used to grasping sword hilts or shield-straps.

One of the Romans, a man from Syracuse, who had once been a gladiator and whose gnarled and scarred face readily told the tale of his grim past, always brought Bran some little titbit from the mess table, and always stayed behind a while to talk to him.

'Come, come, my pretty,' this man would say, 'it's not every dog that sleeps in a Tribune's tent and has a clever doctor and three slave women to attend to him. Get better soon, or I'll be thinking you are dragging out this little sickness so as to get more attention than you deserve!'

Bran did not know what this soldier was saying, but he sensed that the man was good-hearted and meant him well. As he grew stronger, he looked forward to seeing the old gladiator each day. There was an honest smell about him that Bran liked.

But even better were those days when Marcus Titus, the Tribune, was permitted to come off duty. He would stalk into the low red-striped pavilion and would cast aside his heavy helmet as though it were worthless. Then, when he had flung off his long blue cloak and had unbuckled the broad bronze belt which carried his sword and dagger, he would wash his hands and face hurriedly from the bowl that the slave woman held for him, and would sit down in the hay beside Bran, as though at the bedside of a dear comrade-in-arms.

Bran grew to adore this tall man with the firm, gentle voice and the strong warm hands. And as the days wore on, he came to understand much of what the Tribune said to him.

'Tell me, warrior,' Marcus Titus would whisper,' has that old fraud, Klymenes, tended you well today, while I've been fighting my way out of ambushes? If he hasn't, then woe betide the rogue! He shall be made to drink his own vile mixtures and then be set to rowing, with the other slaves, in one of the oyster-boats that ship their delicacies from the shores of Britain to Gaul.'

Klymenes stood by, smiling, and twisted his oiled beard in his long, thin, olive-coloured fingers. He had been with Marcus Titus for five years, had served him as a physician from Palestine to Germany, and knew well enough that the Tribune's bark was worse than his bite. Like all the men of the Ninth, Klymenes would have done anything for this brave young officer who was always first in the battle-ranks when the arrows began to fly and the swords to rise and fall.

The physician said softly, in his Eastern voice, 'The hound has been well-tended, Tribune. So well, indeed, that there must be many hundreds of men in this island —Roman and otherwise—who would willingly change places with him. A warm bed and good food—there are few among the Legions or the tribes who are sure of having such luxuries these days.'

He paused for a moment and then said, 'Indeed, master, since his wounds are now healed and we have put some flesh on those gaunt bones, it is my opinion that the dog could begin to walk again—if only we could find a way of putting some spirit into him. He has suffered much, it seems, and that dulls a creature's spirit. See what you can do, Tribune—you can do most things.'

So Marcus Titus sat beside Bran and fondled him, talking to him on an even tone all the time, the way half-wild creatures like to be addressed. The Roman's voice lulled the hound, but he showed no sign of wishing to move, however much the Tribune tried to persuade him.

At last Marcus Titus said, 'Well, comrade, if you won't walk, I will carry you, since your doctor recommends a breath of fresh air for you.'

The slave women clustered in the doorway saw the great soldier staggering past them, his arms enfolded about the war dog and bearing him as tenderly as a mother holds her baby.

One young Syrian girl said to her companions with a mock sigh, 'How I wish I were in that dog's place! Such a handsome man is our master!'

Marcus Titus heard her, but put on his stern expression of *dignitas*, and passed by without answering. The girl and her companions giggled and ran away, to tell the cooks what their wonderfully crack-brained master was up to!

So the Roman sat with Bran across his knees under an apple-tree. The winter had passed and now the first buds were bursting on the boughs. Soon would come the blossom, and then all the orchards would be dressed in white and pink, like young brides celebrating their marriages in the temples near the Appian Way.

'Ah, my friend,' said Marcus Titus quietly, 'if we ever get back to Rome again, then you will see something. And they'll love you there, a true British war dog! Especially now that your coat has grown long and shaggy again! All things British are the fashion, you know, comrade. Even the great ladies wear the tartans of the tribes and have their hair dyed yellow. Oh, but it will amuse you, my friend! It amuses me!'

He paused a while and then said, 'But you'll like the countryside above Ostia even better. I have a farm there, a white villa set among the cypresses, with the hills behind it and the blue sea before it. My herdsmen are always singing, friend, and my cattle are fat and contented. You'll like that, war dog, I promise you— one of these days, one of these days when this war has worn itself out.'

But Bran did not understand what Marcus Titus was saying. He only knew that if he could not have Gwyn the Golden, then this great strong man who smelled of iron and leather, and whose wrists were circled with gold, was the man for him.

It was while the two were sitting under the apple-tree that the trumpets suddenly howled from behind a spinney, as though giving warning of someone's approach to the encampment.

Two men came riding into view on tall white horses. The Tribune looked up lazily and saw that they were dressed as Legates, officers of a far superior rank to himself. One of them, the more splendidly armed, sat hunched in his saddle as though he were not used to riding. As he came closer, Marcus Titus saw with amazement that this man wore a purple cloak, and instead of a helmet, a narrow gold band about his thin hair.

The Tribune tried to get to his feet, but Bran's weight was too heavy for quick movement and the horsemen were already beside him. The Tribune smiled and bowed his head in deference.

'My lords,' he said, 'as you see, I am prevented from paying you the respect due to you. I beg you, pardon me.'

The Legate with the immense white horsehair plume and the embossed breastplate of gold, stared at the Tribune with wide, red-rimmed eyes. Spittle gathered at the corners of his lips, as though his anger was about to break out.

'By all the gods,' he began, 'but what has the Ninth come to when a Tribune sets a dog before his Emperor!'

The hunched man in the purple cloak shook his head gently and smiled, his sad and ugly face almost pleasant for a moment, and then said, 'Patience, Aulus Plautius! What is a stupid, stuttering old fellow like me worth to a fine young soldier who has a war dog to fondle?'

Marcus Titus stared in bewilderment. So, before him, stood two of the greatest men in the world—the new Emperor Claudius, whom some thought of as a god even; and the General of the Ninth, Aulus Plautius, who had command of many thousand men . . . And he, Marcus Titus, a mere Major, sitting under a tree, playing with a sick dog!

The Tribune said, in some confusion, 'My lord, I have fought for Rome wherever the Eagles have been carried; and so I shall do again, while life is in me and the Empire needs me. I pray you, pardon me for not standing to attention this time.'

The Emperor Claudius nodded, as though he were ruminating over an old poem, or a page of history, for he was well-known as a scholar. Then he said, in his slow and stammering voice, his great Adam's apple bobbing up and down, adding to his grotesque appearance, 'My boy, you are Marcus Titus of Ostia, and the bravest Tribune of a brave Legion. That much I know,

you see. I know also that your dear father, may the gods bless his memory, Senator Marcus Julius, was the man who commanded the Imperial Guard to get rid of Emperor Caligula the madman, and to hoist me on their shoulders in his place. I owe my crown to him, my boy.'

He slipped tiredly from his great horse, flinging the reins to the surprised Aulus Plautius and, hobbling over to where Marcus Titus sat, kneeled down beside him in the heather. With a sly wink, which made him seem funnier than ever, the Emperor went on, 'And what is more, in my young days, when Rome thought I was an idiot and a coward, because I didn't like killing Christians in the arena, or watching the gladiators beating each other's brains out, it was another of your family who took me under her wing and made me feel like a man again—your pretty young aunt, Julia . . . Aye, Julia of the blue eyes. Many was the day we sailed in her little barge along the Tiber, or strolled in the woods above Velitrae.'

His pale eyes stared among the overhanging branches of the apple-tree, and then he said softly, 'Once, in her chariot on the Via Valeria, I made up a poem to her. I can still recall it, Marcus. It went like this . . .'

Aulus Plautius of the Ninth coughed then and began to rattle his bronze sword-sheath against the metal armour of his thigh.

'Emperor,' he said, 'time is passing and we have much to do.'

Claudius smiled at Marcus Titus and patted him on the shoulder. 'You see, boy,' he said, 'my generals give me no peace! I hereby make this vow; if you come alive out of the battle at Mai Dun which is to be soon, and I pray that you do, then I will make *you* a general, Marcus. So I shall be sure of one great officer who will not order me about as though I were a hired spearman from Greece!'

Aulus Plautius coughed again, and stared rigidly above their heads. He was an impatient man who had no time for chatting under apple-trees about the past. To Aulus Plautius there was only the present—with a sharp sword in its hand . . .

The Emperor sighed and got back wearily into the saddle. As the two great ones turned their horses, Aulus Plautius half-turned his stern head and called back to Marcus Titus, 'Tribune, our Second Legion is moving against the fortress of Mai Dun, where that fool Caratacus hopes to make a great stand. But one man travels faster than many, and so I command you to visit this Mai Dun, in whatever disguise you choose, and then to report back to Vespasian, of the Second Legion, on its strength. They must attack at the right time, and in the right place. Is that understood? It is a question of speed; I believe the hothead, Vespasian, is already on the way there!'

Marcus Titus bowed his head. 'It is understood, sir,' he said. 'When am I to make this journey?'

The general snorted and said, 'At the earliest moment, Tribune. There will be no more time for playing with dogs. And do not forget that your mission is a secret one. No one is to know of it—no one. Get there, and get back, for Vespasian will not wait!'

He paused a moment and then said, 'If they catch you, these Celts, it will not be pleasant; you understand that. But on no account are you to give them any details of our forces or positions.'

Marcus Titus looked sharply away from his general, as though these words were insulting. The Emperor Claudius gave a little smile at the young man's annoyance. Then the two rode away.

12 · The Great Fortress

MARCUS TITUS was walking carefully over the far downs. He wore a long and shapeless robe of green wool, covered by a cape and hood of deerskin. At his side hung a well-filled pouch of medicines, about his neck a silver chain, at the end of which dangled a cunningly-carved seal of agate, showing Mithras slaying the bull and so bringing light and health to the world.

All this was appropriate to his new character, that of a wandering physician from southern Gaul. He had served in the Province long enough, in the Station at Lugdunum, and spoke the language well enough to pass even among Gallic farmers for one of themselves. His new name was Dwryd. Aulus Plautius himself had decided on that.

And this Dwryd who had spent his life with weapons now carried none—none save a surgeon's sharp little knife—which might perhaps be put to two uses, at a pinch—and a small green phial of aconite poison, suspended on a thin silken cord inside his robe. This was a last resort, not a weapon to be used against the enemy.

Old Claudius had said, in their final interview before the venture, 'My boy, you are going among a savage and a desperate people. Caratacus and his Catuvellauni are not the ones I fear—they have the noble instincts of true warriors . . . But in their flight from us after the battle for Camulodunum, they have taken up with the western Silures; and they, I fear, are a pitiless folk . . . Scarcely less savage than the day they first left their caves and began to put on human clothing! If the Silures discovered that you are not what you profess, then your end would be a fearsome one. I will not go into details; I will only say that you must carry with you a strong poison which you can slip into your mouth before the Silurian torturers get to work—if the worst comes to the worst.'

So Dwryd of Lugdunum did as his Emperor bade. He also did another thing—he waited long enough in the Roman camp to let his dark-brown and curly beard grow. This not only altered his appearance; it also covered the two callouses on his jawbone, which every Roman soldier had from wearing the tightly-clipping cheek-flaps of the helmet. The Celts, who usually wore helmets without side-guards, knew where to look or where to feel, when they took a disguised prisoner . . .

And while the Tribune's beard grew, Bran became steadily stronger. His hair grew, too, and now he hardly looked like a war dog. In the last few days he hardly left the Roman's side, seeming to sense that his new master was about to leave him.

'Oh, cheer up, boy, for the love of Mithras,' said Marcus Titus one morning when he found the dog lying, nose between paws, his eyes gazing upwards reproachfully. 'I shall soon be back with you! Anyone would think I was going to my death, by the way you stare at me! Here, eat this meat and be happy!'

But Bran would not eat the meat. He would not even drink the warm cow's milk that one of the slave women set down for him in a red dish of Samian pottery.

Marcus Titus left at dawn the next day, before the dog was awake. No one saw him go, not even the sentry at the gate of the oak stockade—he was drowsing gently after a night's watch, leaning on his long javelin, his helmet pushed back for comfort.

The Tribune slid past him, thinking that one day, after all this was over, he would have the man into his tent and speak a few sharp words to him for treating his duties so lightly . . .

Then, a mile from the camp, Marcus Titus was suddenly aware of a rustling and a faint yelping behind him. He drew himself behind a broad oak-tree and waited, his short knife in his hand. But he need not have bothered about wolves or strange hounds . . .

Bran came into view, sniffing and swinging his puzzled head from side to side. The Tribune ran out to meet him and said, 'Why, you old rogue! You are hardly better yet! Why do you wish to come on this dangerous mission when you could be lying warm and safe beside the camp-fire?'

Bran leaned against the Tribune's leg and gave a great sigh, as though, now that he had found what he had lost, he would never let it go again.

Marcus Titus knew enough about the loyalty of war dogs not to try sending the faithful creature back. He scratched his dark head and said ruefully, 'Very well, if the gods will it . . . But I did not bargain for this, dear friend.'

There was something else Marcus Titus did not bargain for; three nights out, lying in a small coppice under an overhanging rock, he was wakened from his sleep by a loud baying, and sat up to see Bran defying two great wolves, just beyond the light of the small fire.

When these hunters saw that the hound now had an active companion, they turned tail and slunk away into the shadows. The Tribune stroked Bran's head and said, 'Thank you, comrade! Now I have my answer—if you are strong enough to outface such a pair of ambushers, then you are strong enough to come with me to the west. Sit down, boy, and we will have a little feast to celebrate your return to health.'

So Marcus Titus piled up more brushwood on the fire, and the two ate sheep-meat and drank goat's milk from a leather flask which the Tribune carried over his shoulder, after the manner of wandering men.

Bran's strength came back to him, day by day, as they made their way towards the west, and the Tribune delighted to see his companion loping beside him now, almost as though he had never lain at the doors of death —apart from the deep scars which still showed on his sides and which would never again be covered by hair.

And so, two weeks out from the camp of the Ninth Legion, they first saw signs of the men they had come to seek. One evening, just as the sun was setting, they came out of a narrow gully to see, black against the sky, a shaggy horseman above them. His pointed lance and the horns of his helmet gave him a strange and fearsome look.

The Tribune whispered, 'One of the Catuvellauni, my friend. One of your own folk. Go with him if you wish; you have my permission.'

But Bran only growled up at the horseman, and showed his long white fangs. The horse snorted in fear and edged away. Its rider called down something which Marcus Titus did not understand, and then cantered away, beyond the ridge.

Half a mile farther on, in a wood where the holly trees grew thickly, four tribesmen ran out from behind a rock and drew their short bows at the Tribune's chest.

He held up his hand, palm outward, to signify that he came in peace, and called out in his thickest Gallic accent, 'You must be very healthy men to think of killing a doctor, my lads! I am Dwryd of Lugdunum, and an expert in diseases of the eyes and the stomach. I thought you might have some use for me.'

The Tribune knew well enough what he was about, for in recent times there had been much inflammation of the eye among those tribesmen who lived near the coastal marshes. Moreover, certain of the Syrian contingents of the Legions, long practised in desert warfare, had taken to poisoning the wells after they had filled their own barrels and wineskins—a form of attack to which Celts were unused, and the resulting pangs of which had struck the terror of magic into the more superstitious of the clans who had suffered.

A war-scarred man who wore his thick brown hair bound round with gold wire came forward, a short dirk in his right hand. He stopped a yard or two from Marcus Titus and, with a violent gesture towards Bran, said, 'You may be a good doctor, Dwryd of Lugdunum, but we do not trust Gauls in this land now. And we are doubly unsure of men who come with a British war dog at their heels.'

The Roman laughed and flung his arms wide, as though he had nothing to fear. 'But, my dear man,' he said, 'who can blame a doctor—Gaul or not—from plying his trade wherever there are patients to be had? I tell you, the Roman fools have doctors enough; a poor wanderer like me stands no chance against all these Egyptians and Greeks who fuss round the Tribunes with their potions and salves and herb poultices! As for the dog—I ask you, do you know any way of driving off a big hound like this when once he has decided to follow you? Tell me the answer, and I'll listen to it, I promise you!'

The men lowered their bows and began to nod and laugh; they knew only too well how obstinate these war dogs were. Besides, they liked this big merry Gaul, who didn't show any sign of fear although he carried no weapons.

Their leader pushed his broad dirk into his belt and said gruffly, 'You smell all right to me, outlander. And we do need a doctor, that I must admit. As for the dog, he looks the sort we need. The King will accept him as a gift from you, if he is in the right humour. Come, man, we will take you to the great fortress—but one word of warning; if you as much as speak out of turn, you are a dead man, doctor or not. We are the King's killers and must guard him in this strange land, now that the Roman swine have rooted us out of our own place.'

The Tribune bowed his head and smiled, as though quite at ease; yet, beneath that rough robe of wool his heart was now thudding violently.

They set off into the dusk, and after much turning and twining, through woods, round rocks, and along little streams, they came to a great mound that stood high against the evening sky.

'That is Mai Dun, the Great Fortress,' said one of the tribesmen, pointing with his spear.

Marcus Titus said with a smile, 'From all its many walls and stockades, I would guess that it is as hard to get out of it as into it, my friend!'

The man laughed and nodded. 'This is our fortress against the Roman pigs,' he said. 'If they break us here, then it must be the will of the gods. We must find another battlefield.'

He halted a while, then added, 'But I do not think they will take this place.'

The Tribune looked about him and had to agree. Row upon row of long mound-walls stretched up the steep hill to its flat summit; and there stood an oak stockade as high as two men, its stakes set so closely that only a little child could push between them. And everywhere along the walls were tribesmen, their javelins so thickly stacked that the hill had something of the look of a gigantic porcupine.

The party passed through the first gate, a massive thing of thick trunks, which needed six men to unbar and open it. Then they began their long and winding climb up the hill, between the interlocking walls. Marcus Titus was a soldier of long experience, and his quick eyes told him, even in the twilight, that a single file of men, even hardened legionaries, would be cut to pieces before they could gain the summit. He wished he had a trained carrier-pigeon to send back this news to the Emperor and to Vespasian. Suddenly, he felt very lonely and cut off; now there was only his dog to keep him company in this savage and foreign place. And what of Bran? Even he, once more among his own folk, might forget his friendship to a Roman . . .

Fires burned everywhere on the hill-top; men, women and children clustered about the many wattle huts, laughing, singing, playing, eating. Hens clucked, cows bellowed, horses neighed and pawed the hard ground. Smoke hung everywhere, for it was a strangely still night; and, now that they were on the flattened hill-top, Marcus Titus saw the last dying rays of the sun, sinking somewhere out in the western sea. It cast a foreboding red-gold glow across the darkening wooded land, especially when seen through the smoke from the fires.

In the middle of the flattened summit stood a tall

circular place of wood, built much after the Roman manner, with pillars. But these pillars were of oak, the rough bark still hanging on them. And nailed the length of each one were whitened skulls.

The Tribune lowered his eyes with a sensation of disgust. These folk were savages, barbarians, and no

good could come of taking their land from them and trying to show them Roman ways, civilized ways . . . This, also, he would have written to Claudius, if that imaginary pigeon had been at hand to carry the message.

'Come, doctor,' said the leader of the band, pushing the Roman hard in the back with the butt of his spear, 'here is the King's house. All strangers must bow the knee to Caratacus.'

The single great room of the King's house was lit only with rush tapers, burning in oil-bowls. A smoking fire stood in the middle of the room, and beside this, on a rough bench covered with sheep-skins, sat the King. Marcus Titus gazed at him in wonder before he fell to his knees before him. Could this man really be a King? In Italy, or even southern Gaul, one would have taken him for a small farmer, a crofter who could scarcely make ends meet. His golden hair was uncombed and hung, in greasy locks, about his sagging shoulders. His tunic was of horse-hide, much scraped and rubbed. About his long legs he wore coarse wool breeches, bound round with thongs. Only the heavy gold spirals about his arms and the broad bronze collar, set with garnets and jet, told that he was a person of some quality. Those, and the great iron sword in its enamelled scabbard, leaning against the rude oak bench.

The Roman took in all this at one glance. Then he had something else to occupy his mind, for the King suddenly said, 'The world has become a strange place, Dwryd of Lugdunum, when a travelling doctor must

needs make his rounds with a war dog of the Catuvellauni. I know this hound, doctor, in spite of his long
coat. If you will feel beneath the hair on his right ear,
you will find my own brand. I last saw him, fighting
bravely beside my own chariot, outside Camulodunum.
How do you explain that, Gaul?'

He stared at Marcus Titus with wide pale eyes,
fixedly, as though he could see into his very heart. Even
the brave Tribune felt a momentary shiver of anxiety
under this strange King's scrutiny. But he stared back
as firmly as he could, and even smiled.

'The dog followed me, lord,' he said. 'That is all I
know.'

Caratacus turned towards the dog and said softly,
'Bran, boy, come to your King now. Come, Bran, you
are home again.'

13 · Strange Meeting

FOR an instant, the dog seemed about to move towards the King, like a creature in a trance. Then, with a sudden shake of the head, he shattered the last vestiges of his loyalty for Caratacus and, drawing back his lips, began to snarl, the hackles rising on his broad shoulders.

The King stared at Bran in astonishment. His mouth opened to speak, but no words came from it. His eyes widened and something like fear showed beside the anger in them.

'By Mabon!' he said thickly. 'But a dog which turns against his own King is better dead!'

A guard who stood by the door ran forward, his short throwing-spear raised.

'It is the King's will!' he cried, and drew back his hand for the cast.

Suddenly a red cloth seemed to come down before the eyes of Marcus Titus. No longer the cool, controlled Roman, he shuffled forward three paces and then hit the guard with a punch that Rome's finest gladiator would have envied. He felt the jarring pain of that blow as far as his elbow, but smiled with a grim satisfaction to see the man's legs crumple to let him fall headlong among the rushes, his spear flying wide.

'To me, Bran!' he yelled, every bit as wild as a Celt. The great hound responded, even as the curtains parted and a group of men rushed forward with drawn swords.

What happened then was like a dream—all confusion and shouting. The Roman felt himself flung sideways with a blow on the temple from an axe-shaft. For a second, he saw Bran snapping and tearing above him, and heard cries of fear and pain from those who had run in too recklessly.

Then all cleared again, and the Tribune felt himself being hauled to his feet roughly. Two men were holding Bran down; three others were dragging the Roman's arms back; the King, Caratacus, had gone from the dimly-lit room—and now another man faced Marcus Titus. A short, swarthy-skinned man whose black hair was fastened up with white bone pins. He wore a thick bearskin and his cheekbones were streaked with bands of woad. In his hand he held a double-headed axe of stone.

Marcus Titus gazed at this man with gathering contempt.

'Mathonwy the traitor!' he said, through clenched teeth. 'So, we meet again in different circumstances, eh? Last time you were selling information to the Roman Ambassador in Gaul; today you profess to be the friend of that poor deluded King, Caratacus!'

Mathonwy smiled slowly, showing his worn-down and yellow teeth. Then, almost leisurely, he struck the Roman across the face with the flat of his axe. The Tribune could not protect himself, since his hands were held behind him. He swayed and almost fell. Only his pride, his courage, his Roman will kept him from falling senseless.

Then, from the rushes on the floor, came a great baying. Bran whirled like a high wind, flinging the tribesmen from him. Then suddenly he was at his master's side, rearing up and slashing with his fearsome fangs.

As the men who held Marcus Titus turned and fled before this onslaught, sly Mathonwy drew back a pace and raised his war-axe high above his head, his broad and painted face alight with cruelty. This was the dog who had tumbled him in the dust, before all the noblemen of Camulodunum, at the testing, long before. Now was the hour of vengeance, he thought!

But Bran had caught the scent of this man only a moment earlier, and what he had once begun he now longed to finish. Coming in at an oblique angle, he took the axe-blow on the shoulder and not on the skull. It was a glancing stroke which stung but did not cripple.

Bran leaped high as the man swung back to strike again. Marcus Titus heard the shrill cry as the war dog found his target. He heard the stone axe fall with a clatter to the floor.

And then, even as Mathonwy tottered, clutching at his throat, the air was filled as with the buzzing of a thousand hornets. A great weight seemed to crash against the roof-tree of the King's house, bringing down timbers and rushes in a headlong cascade. A boulder as big as a hill pony thundered to the floor, rocking the very foundations of the house.

Outside, men were shouting, 'The siege engines! The siege engines! The Romans have come!'

Marcus Titus staggered to the shattered doorway, Bran at his heels, and saw the havoc and confusion that the great mangonels were causing. Boulders showered down upon the summit of Mai Dun, crushing the stockades and crumbling the earthen walls. Men ran hither and thither, buckling on their armour; women screamed and children sobbed. Now the bright fires were all put out, and the humped Dun was left in semi-darkness.

Far down the slope the Roman war-horns howled. The Tribune paused a moment, the hairs at the nape of his neck prickling with excitement.

'They have come indeed, Bran,' he said. 'Vespasian has not waited for my news! With the help of Mithras, the Light-giver, we may yet be safe!'

As he spoke, the words of a song floated up the hill, making itself heard even above the screams and the savage war-cries of the Celts. A few of his own Legion must be marching with the Second!

> '*When we marched out from Tarraco,*
> *The new swords in our hands,*
> *The fine Centurion, he said*
> *We'd kiss a thousand girls!*

> *But all we've kissed is northern snow,*
> *Or lain in southern sands;*
> *The lads we marched with first are dead*
> *After a thousand miles!'*

Marcus Titus, Tribune of the Ninth, the 'Hispana,' drew himself up straight, no longer a shambling physician from Lugdunum, but a soldier once again.

He took Bran by the hair at the neck and whispered urgently, 'Come, boy! It's now or never! They may not recognize us in this confusion!'

So the two set off down the steep hill, winding in and out among the mounds and walls. Once, a shaggy-haired chieftain called out for the Roman to stop and help him with an overturned cart, but the Tribune called back a mocking apology in Gallic, and ran on. Once, at the corner of a wall, man and dog plunged through a group of Silures who were crouched over a small fire, lighting fire-arrows; but they took Marcus to be a young warrior of the Catuvellauni, anxious to be at the throat of the invading enemy.

So, down and down they ran, until, less than thirty paces before them, they saw the first rank of the Romans, marching steadily along, under the heavy barrage laid down by the mangonels. At their head was a rough figure on a horse—Vespasian of the Second, his helmet on the back of his head, his sword out, beating time to the marching song. The Tribune had seen him ride like this before, in a Triumph along the Appian Way.

Marcus Titus yelled out, 'I am coming, General!'

At that moment the first great volley of arrows came down from the hill-top. The sound they made was that of an eagle's pinions as he swoops above his quarry, a deep droning rustle, full of hatred and of terror.

Marcus Titus saw a grim warrior-smile on the

94

General's face, then he saw men and horses falling to left and right, caught in that narrow defile among the mound walls.

A second later he felt two great blows, in the small of the back and in the right leg. It was as though a giant had struck him out of the darkness. He fell headlong into a greater darkness, at the feet of the General's horse.

Quickly the first Company reformed and put up a shield-wall to protect their wounded.

The General, Vespasian, got down wearily from his horse and watched while the surgeon cut the arrows from the unconscious Tribune's back and leg.

'Will he live, man?' he asked, anxiously.

The surgeon wiped his hands and nodded, briefly.

'He should do,' he said. 'He has a constitution like a stallion. But this will be the end of soldiering for him now; that leg will always be stiff from this night on.'

The General pursed his lips and said, 'He has served Rome well. He deserves a little peace at last. My friend, Aulus Plautius, thinks very highly of him, I understand.'

Then, turning, he called to his scribe and said, 'See that the Tribune's honourable discharge is made out this very evening. He shall sail on the next ship back to Rome. And see that this dog of his goes with him. They shall not be separated by me, after what they have been through together.'

Much later, when the fortress was taken and the Second had set their tents upon the hill-top, Vespasian sent for a young woman who had been captured after the battle of Camulodunum. She was pretty and golden-haired, and still wore the bracelets and neck-rings of a princess.

'Lady,' he said to her, as politely as his gruff voice would let him, 'here is the Tribune I mentioned to you yesterday, the one who was spying for us. Will you sail with him to Rome and tend his wounds?'

She nodded and said, 'Yes, General. He looks to be a brave man. But I would go with him in any case, for Bran loves him, and Bran was once my own brother's dog, in the good days before war cast its shadow across our land.'

Vespasian rose from his stool and took the girl's hands in his own.

'Lady Myrina,' he said, 'I am obliged to you, and I thank you. One day, when the world is a gentle place again, I will come to Ostia myself and visit you. May the gods deal kindly with you, on the voyage and ever after.'

Myrina, sister of Gwyn the Golden, bowed her head and then went from the tent. Bran, lying beside his new master's pallet of straw, gazed after her with large brown eyes. He had known her since he had been a puppy, and now, by some strange sense unknown to man, he realized that he was to be with her once again. His great shaggy head sank gently between his paws. Gazing upwards at his master's pale face, he licked his still hand, as though to tell him that all would be well now.

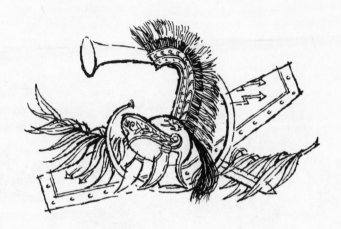

14 · The Crossing

BUT all did not go so well on that crossing from
Britain to Gesoriacum, in Gaul.

True enough, the *Augustus*, the Roman supply-ship
that the friends sailed in, had two banks of oars *and* a
great sail to help it along. At the after-end, it even had a
roofed cabin that was warm and snug when the bitter
salty winds snarled across the Channel and the high
green waves beat over the gunwales. But it was a high-
built vessel and tended to wallow a little. It was not
meant for speed, but moved with a stately, even pompous, Roman dignity—which was well enough for born
sailors, but less good for such as had spent their lives on
solid earth.

Just before dawn, on the second day out against con-

trary winds, three dark longships, rowed only by a dozen oars and so low in the water that every wave seemed to smother them, came out of the swirling mists, the greedy gulls squawking and wheeling above them.

Myrina, feeling sick and leaning against the prow of the Roman ship, saw them first and knew what they were, so black and snake-like, so swift and silent in their approach.

She called back to the captain, a burly Spaniard from Gades, 'Look, man, away to the steerboard! Those three are Frisian ships. I have seen craft like that before, lying off our coasts, waiting for merchant-men. They call themselves the Wolves of the Sea. We can expect no mercy from them.'

The captain shrugged his heavy shoulders, but he did

not reply to the girl; he seemed to think that beneath his dignity, since he had recently become a Roman citizen. Instead, he muttered to the man who was beating out the rowing-pace on a flat drum, 'These Celts! These Celts! They are so befogged with their witchcraft and tree-gods, you can't knock any sense into them. Sea wolves indeed! Why, I've sailed against the cleverest pirates the African coast can breed—and I'm still here!'

The pace-maker laughed deep in his hairy chest, not because he was brave but because he did not wish to offend this hot-tempered man from Gades, who had a bad reputation among sailormen for being a keel-hauling bully.

Myrina called out again, 'See, they are closing in! They are on all sides now!'

The Spanish captain blew his nose loudly and began to whistle a mocking tune. It was the last thing he ever did, because an arrow suddenly appeared in his neck and he never got the tune finished. The shrill whistling stopped on a high, uncertain note. Then the man who did not fear the Africans crumpled up, fell to his knees like someone saying his prayers, and gently slid to the boards beneath the prow-platform.

The slaves who were rowing began to gabble in their different languages, but the frightened pace-maker yelled at them to quicken their speed and to keep calm. The steerboard-man, who could see everything now, called out that there was just a chance of the *Augustus* breaking through, if the pace held.

One rower, a long-faced wrestler from Sicily, pulled so hard then that he snapped the worn ash-shaft of his oar. This flung him backwards and so toppled all behind him from their low benches. The *Augustus* shuddered and began to swing about.

It was then that the first Frisian boat ran in, almost alongside. Myrina saw that it carried a dozen men, ragged and salt-caked, laughing all over their red and bearded faces. To them, it was a great joke for a proud Roman ship to cripple itself out in the little Channel, and on a day that was not especially rough.

But Roman ships are not so easily taken. The steerboard-man swung his broad oar round in a contrary motion and the galley seemed to snort and rear like a horse as it obeyed the summons. Or perhaps it was like a heavy ox that changes its direction without warning and tramples the dog running beside it.

Horrified, Myrina saw that the *Augustus* had almost jumped round in the sea and now had swung half-over the first Frisian boat. She saw the pirates' faces, which had been so merry before, so confident; but whose laughter had suddenly changed to a terrified shouting.

There was a sickening crunch, and then the *Augustus* was sailing free again, though in a different direction. Behind her a low black hulk bobbed on the grey-green sea, raw hands clutching at its shattered planks. The waiting gulls had come lower now and were shrieking like maniacs.

One of the five Roman soldiers who acted as guards to the *Augustus* stared down towards the water, smiling grimly, and said, 'When will they learn, these savages, that no one touches Rome without getting his fingers burned!'

Myrina turned away from the dreadful scene and ran as fast as she could along the swaying timbers of the ship, to the little cabin where Marcus Titus lay, his wounded leg in splints.

Bran rested, nose between paws, at the foot of the Tribune's narrow, hide-thonged bed. When the dog saw Myrina, he rose and gazed up at her with great puzzled eyes; but she paid little attention to Bran now—her mission was with his master.

'Tribune,' she said, 'we are being attacked by pirates —three Frisian longships. At least, there *were* three— but now there are only two. The *Augustus* trampled one of them down.'

The Roman nodded, his handsome face grave. 'I know,' he said. 'I felt the blow we gave them. I thought the floor would give beneath me with the strain. But we should soon come within sight of the lighthouse at Gesoriacum. There are always Roman patrol-boats in those waters. Perhaps these savages will leave us soon. It would be better for us all if they did.'

He had hardly finished when the *Augustus* swung round again, the steerboard-man hoping to repeat his earlier victory; but this time luck did not lie with Rome. Even as the unwieldy ship heaved about, a sudden vicious gust of wind caught the drenched and top-heavy sail, twisting it in the opposite direction. There was an ear-splitting crash, and then the great mast gave and came toppling down, its crow's-nest hitting the sea with a loud smack.

The *Augustus* heeled over and for a while seemed to hover above the water, as though she might turn turtle. Slaves shouted out in alarm, fearing to go down into the sea chained to their benches. Titus himself would have tumbled from his bed with the ship's sudden heave if Myrina had not flung herself against him. Even Bran, usually so firm and so sure-footed, was hurled against the cabin wall, growling and shaking his great fierce head in bewilderment.

Now the pace-maker had stopped beating his drum, for the oars on one side were deep in the sea, while those on the other flailed helplessly in the air, like the legs of a crab.

The soldiers ran between the rowers' benches, knocking off the shackles which held the poor wretches prisoner. Many of them, as soon as they were free, turned and leapt silently into the foamy waves, hoping to throw themselves on the mercy of the pirates rather than risk capsizing in the *Augustus*.

But the two remaining Frisian boats had drawn away now, hoping to watch the Romans die from a safe distance. Few slaves reached the Frisians, and those who did quickly learned that those sea-wolves had no wish to take any prisoners that day.

Myrina, who was standing at the cabin door, covered her eyes with her hands and sobbed, 'Oh, the brutes! The savage brutes!'

Amidships, two legionaries were attacking the splintered mast with axes, trying to get the *Augustus* free from the water-soaked wood and canvas, and that mass of cordage which now enveloped the ship like a gigantic spider-web.

The steerboard-man yelled out, 'Level the load! All of you, run to the uppermost side, or we shall turn over!'

The slaves and merchants who had been flung down towards the sea now began to clamber upwards over bales of merchandise, kegs of oysters and stacks of timber. For a moment the *Augustus* righted herself, and the drenched passengers even began to smile again and to slap one another on the back in relief.

Then suddenly, his dark eyes wide, his red finger pointing, the pace-maker shouted, 'Look! We are stove in! That mast has sprung the timbers along one side!'

Just below the water-line the grey-green sea was pushing its way into the stricken ship. At first it came in between the planks with a froth like the white plumes of a row of cavalry horses; then it seemed to settle down and well aboard, as though the sea was quietly confident that the *Augustus* was a doomed vessel.

Men stared down, speechless, as the water swirled round their ankles, carrying straw, trussed chickens and rolls of linen with it. Three stallions at the after-end, being taken as a present from Vespasian to the Governor of Puteoli, began to scream with terror and to kick their stalls to splinters.

Marcus Titus made a grimace of pain, then reached down for his broad-bladed sword. 'Take this, Myrina,' he said, 'and cut the halters of those poor beasts. At least, they should have a chance to swim for their lives.'

Myrina, who had lived her life among horses and loved them as did all Celts, drew the heavy blade from its scabbard and, hitching up her woollen skirts to leave her legs free, splashed away from the cabin.

'Look after the Roman until I come back, Bran,' she called over her shoulder.

The Tribune smiled and reached out to pat the hound's shaggy head.

'At least we'll go down like soldiers, Bran,' he said quietly. 'We won't squeal for mercy, eh, boy?'

Then suddenly Myrina was back again, breathing hard and smiling, her fair hair drenched and plastered across her face.

'Tribune,' she gasped, 'we are saved. Four Roman patrol-boats are heading towards us. They can be no more than a bow-shot away from us now. You see, I said a prayer to Belatucader as I ran to cut the horses loose—and now look what has happened! Our Celtic gods have heard. Now do you still believe that we are barbarians?'

Marcus Titus scratched his ear and smiled to himself. Then he held out his hand for the great sword.

'I hope you didn't hack the edge on those iron halter-rings,' he said, very calmly. 'This sword belonged to my father and has never needed to be sharpened yet. It is a special iron that holds an edge for a hundred years, the smiths say—that is, if you don't lend it to a woman!'

As the Roman boats nosed alongside the *Augustus*, Myrina screwed up her eyes and pinched in her lips, doing her best to look angry.

'Men!' she said with a little snort. 'They are always the same! They think more of their toy swords than the really *important* things!'

Behind her back, Marcus Titus winked at Bran and, for an instant in the shadows of the cabin, it almost seemed that the war dog winked back at him . . .

But it was just a trick of the light, no doubt.

15 · Gesoriacum

BEFORE taking the wagon-train down through Gaul, the Tribune, Myrina and Bran stayed for some days in the bustling port of Gesoriacum, to which the patrol-boats had brought them.

A clever young Sicilian doctor who examined Marcus advised this period of rest, since the Tribune's wounds had become inflamed during that voyage across the stormy Channel.

They lodged in a tavern almost under the shadow of the gaunt stone lighthouse which the mad Emperor Caligula had erected there some years earlier. The land-lord was a merry-faced man, a Belgian who didn't care whether his guests were Romans or Celts, as long as they paid their reckoning and started no fights in his tavern.

He was glad to have such a distinguished man as the Tribune for a guest, and saw to it that the serving-maids put extra blankets on the bed to keep the Roman warm. He had a specially soft spot for Bran, also, because, as he said, no wandering German robbers would dare to break into the tavern at night, with such a watch-dog on the premises.

As for Myrina, the landlord gave one look at the chiselled gold neck-band she wore—then almost fell on his knees before her in adoration.

Marcus Titus was greatly amused at this. 'Why, look at the fellow,' he said. 'He's babbling like a fool, and staring at you as though you might be a goddess come down to walk the earth again!'

Myrina, who could put on astonishing airs if given the chance, curled a strand of her golden hair about her finger, and said quite simply, 'He knows I am a princess. He is a man of good sense—and good manners.'

The Tribune, who by now was beginning to feel quite well again, answered jokingly, 'Yes, that's all very well, but I am a Roman officer. Does that not count for any-thing in this fellow's eyes?'

Myrina preened herself as she walked to the lattice window and pretended to look down into the market square below. Quietly she said, 'I have yet to hear that a rough soldier, Roman or not, stands higher than the sister of a man like Gwyn, who is second-cousin to Caratacus himself.'

The Tribune looked away and smiled a little sadly.

It would be unkind to tell the girl that she came from a conquered people; that she was, to all intents and purposes, little more than a slave captured in battle.

Instead, he put on a solemn face and said, 'Forgive me, princess! Please don't have me whipped—until my leg is better!'

Then Myrina turned round and laughed out loud, running to the Roman and making a great housewifely show of tucking the blankets round him.

'Why, you silly Roman goose!' she said. Then she stopped, a serious look on her face, for she had remembered that among her own folk, the goose, like the hare, was an almost sacred creature and not to be spoken of carelessly.

'See that you keep warm, Tribune,' she said at last. 'You men can be so stupid when you are ill. My brother broke his arm once, out hunting, and we had such trouble with him because he would go out in the cold before it was properly healed again.'

Marcus bowed his head solemnly, but winked at Bran from the shelter of the blankets.

'I hear and obey, princess,' he said.

Myrina took a wicker basket from the hook on the plaster wall. 'You had better,' she said, 'because I am going down to the market now, before the best things are sold. If you wish to eat and so keep your strength up, then I must go bargaining for you. Bran will stand guard until I return. I am a quick bargainer, so I shall not be long. When people see this gold ring round my neck, they stand back and let me go first. I shall soon be back.'

But she was not soon back. Morning turned to midday, and then to afternoon. Marcus Titus fidgeted, watching the sunlight creep across the wall of his room. At last he could stand it no longer. Then he knocked with a staff on the wooden floor of the bedroom and the landlord came running up, red-faced and anxious.

'What is it, my lord?' he gasped, thinking that the Roman had taken a turn for the worse.

'The girl, Myrina, is not back,' answered the Tribune. 'She went to the market square this morning and has not returned.'

The landlord stared out of the window, his face stiff and masklike. He knew well enough that Myrina was a slave; so many of his own folk were slaves these days and he was familiar with such things. In his mind he pictured the pretty young girl running away from her Roman master, running back to her own people, perhaps, or to friends who would hide her until better days came. But it was not his place to give the girl away. He liked this big, brave Roman well enough—but he respected Myrina even more.

At last he said, falteringly, 'It often takes time—even for a pretty lady—to bargain with these stall-holders, sir. You see, many of them are outlanders, not *proper* folk like us Gauls, not law-keepers. Many of them come from as far away as the East, and have little respect for our women, even for our noblewomen. You will see, my lord, she has gone to another market and so is delayed, that is all.'

The Tribune knew well enough what was passing in the man's mind; he had lived among Celts long enough to think as they did. Now he gave an impatient snort and began to lever himself up in bed.

'Here, fellow,' he said, 'help me on to my feet and reach me my sword. If it's the last thing I do, I'll go down and find her, crippled or not. Apart from my dog, Myrina is the dearest friend I have, and I'll not have her bullied by any stall-holder. Come, give me my sword, man! Don't stand there, chuntering like a pig!'

The landlord gasped in astonishment. If anyone else had called him a pig, he would have struck the man down with a tankard or a ladle. But this Roman was different.

'My lord,' he stammered, 'I did not know . . . I thought you regarded her as a slave. I thought . . .'

'Slave!' roared the Tribune, struggling to get off the bed. 'Have you lost what few senses the gods gave you? Myrina is so dear to me that, one day, if she will be gracious enough to listen to me, I will make her my wife and will get Roman citizenship for her.'

The landlord smiled at last, a proud smile, as though he was happy to belong to the same folk as Myrina, happy also to serve such a Roman as Marcus Titus.

'Lord,' he said, 'you are not ready to go out with a sword after the lady. It is my place to do that for you. I will gather my four sons, and we will search every inch of this town—if we have to tear it stone from stone. We will find the dear lady and bring her back safely to you. I swear it.'

But, in the end, it was not the landlord and his four big-shouldered sons who found Myrina. It was Bran, who had followed them, sniffing, out of the tavern.

His sudden frantic yelping led them to an old and disused stable beyond the harbour. His long bared fangs quickly frightened away the two stubble-bearded Germans who sat outside the hanging door. His keen nose guided the searchers to the heap of damp straw, where Myrina lay, her hands and feet bound with ship's rope.

And when the landlord had undone the gag about her mouth, Myrina bent over and kissed Bran again and again. 'Bran, boy!' she said. 'Lovely boy! They were going to put me on a ship and sell me in the north, among the sea-rovers there. Oh, Bran, dear boy!'

While his sons stood back, their heads bowed in respect, the landlord helped Myrina to her feet.

'Dear lady,' he whispered, 'the Tribune sent us out looking for you. He is half-crazed with grief to think you might be lost. Do you know, lady, he loves you! Yes, he wants to marry you and make you a Roman, like himself. Oh lady, if I could have got my hands on those Germans, I would have. . .'

But Myrina was looking at him with that strange stiff smile again, like the image of a goddess. He drew back from her, his head bowed.

'I beg your pardon, lady,' he mumbled. 'I let my tongue run away with me.'

Myrina said nothing, but walked past him out of the stable, Bran close at her heels. At the tottering door she turned and said lightly, 'I don't mind so much that those Germans tried to capture me. What I do mind about is that I've lost my basket and all the meat and vegetables. Now the Tribune will go short of his supper. He will have no great opinion of me as a housewife, after this.'

The landlord ran after her and said, 'Lady, I have meat and vegetables enough for all of us, in my kitchen. You shall have them, and welcome. I am only glad to be of service to such as you.'

Myrina inclined her golden head slightly and said, 'We thank you, landlord. Of course, the Tribune will wish to pay fairly for what he has. He is a Roman, you understand.'

The landlord's sons shook their tousled heads and made sly grimaces to each other. The eldest said in a whisper to the others, 'What can you make of them— these noblewomen and these Romans? They seem to belong to another world!'

The younger brother said, 'I think I can understand their dog—and that's about all!'

But at this moment Bran gave him such a look that the boy began to whistle and kick a pebble, as though he had never spoken at all.

Later, while Myrina was upstairs, serving hot soup to the Tribune, the landlord said to his sons, 'They are wonderful folk, lads, but, praise to the gods, the wagon-train will set off southwards the day after tomorrow, to carry them to Rome. Then, perhaps, we can live like ordinary common folk once more! Being under the same roof as such great ones is a strain—especially when they have a dog that understands everything you say!'

16 · The Farm above Ostia

IT was early summer in the gentle uplands above Ostia.
Five years had passed as swiftly as a sunlit day—as
they do when there are houses and fields and cattle and
children to attend to.

The farm villa was a pretty place. The approaching
visitor, who climbed the steep path up to it, saw first a
high white wall that ran round the house, in a square.
Above this wall swayed a row of dark and graceful

cypresses which moved in every breeze from the blue
sea below. Between the trees rose the red-tiled roof of
the house. Passing through the gate, which was never
barred, the visitor found himself in a quiet courtyard,
where gaily-plumaged birds fluttered in their cages and
great carp swam lazily in the clear waters of a pool, set
about with ornamental urns and bright red flowers. The
house itself was solid and square, its white façade de-
corated with a row of fluted columns, after the old
Greek manner.

In the shelter of these columns sat the man who had
once been a soldier, and was now a farmer. He had his
right leg stretched out before him, supported on a
gilded stool, for since that fearful night at Mai Dun he
had been lame, in spite of everything good Klymenes
could do. But Marcus Titus was not the man to let such
a small mishap trouble him. Other men had far worse
wounds; and many men were dead now, men of the
Ninth and of the Second, which was worst of all. . .

Marcus Titus was trying to read a book about agri-
culture, but this was not easy for a soldier who had
been away from books so long. Besides, there was
another distraction; his lovely young wife, Myrina, sat
only four paces from him, her corn-coloured hair now
dressed in the Roman fashion, with ribbons and ringlets, trying to learn Latin. The scribe who struggled to
teach her seemed at his wit's end.

'No, no, my dear lady,' he said, almost clenching his
fists in despair. 'You must place your lips so—and
speak lightly, not back in the throat as you do in your
own language!'

Myrina stamped with impatience and flung her book on to the mosaic pavement. 'My own language is a good one,' she said. 'It is the language of Kings, my man!'

Marcus Titus sighed with mock-weariness and closed his own book. 'Dear one,' he said, 'you make a bad pupil, I fear. Try to be patient. Surely, if I can learn Celtic, then you can master Latin.'

'Oh, fish-hooks!' she said, tossing her golden curls. 'You talk like a school-master, Marcus! I tell you, all our peasants talk Celtic to me. They can understand me.'

Her husband nodded and smiled. 'Of course they do,' he said. 'They ruin you because they adore you, my pretty.'

'And my son Caracalla understands me.'

'Yes, my love—but he can speak either language without bothering which one it is. I think he talks Roman by day and dreams Celtic by night.'

'And Bran understands me. What do you say to that, my fierce husband?'

Marcus Titus rose from his chair stiffly and flung down his book.

'Bran would understand you if you did no more than raise an eyebrow,' he said. 'He thinks you are a goddess, Myrina. Indeed, you have quite spoiled him as a war dog, alas! Now he would much rather help get in the sheep, or watch beside the cradle of our new baby. Poor Bran—what have you come to, my dear fellow?'

Myrina stood beside her husband and pointed.

'That's what he has come to, my pompous lord,' she said, in her teasing voice. 'Look well, Tribune!'

Beyond the white wall, among the sheep and the growing lambs, raced a great black hound and a lithe golden-haired boy. The still air was filled with their barking and shouting. White doves rose from the red roof-top in surprise; old ewes turned their lazy heads to watch the two go by. A stallion in the stables began to whinny and paw the ground, as though he was anxious to run with them, too.

'Come, lordly one,' said Myrina with a gentle smile, 'we will go down into the orchard and watch these two at their play.'

Holding his arm, she walked slowly beside the limping Roman.

As they stood beneath the overhanging and laden boughs, Marcus Titus said softly, 'When we send him to the academy in Rome, they will not let him wear those gaudy tartans and great cloak brooches, my dear. He will have to dress Roman-style, soberly. This place will be quiet when he goes.'

Myrina gave a little sniff, then put on a bright smile. 'Don't be such an old raven,' she said. 'He will come back for the holidays. Besides, don't forget, his little sister, Rhiannon, will soon be running about the place with Bran, screaming her lovely dark head off!'

The Roman smiled and nodded. 'It is strange,' he said. 'One dark, and one golden. It is as though our two peoples have mingled in peace, like brother and sister.'

Even as he spoke, little Caracalla burst through the bushes, waving his wooden sword, his hair and short cloak flying. At his heels, running carefully so as not to trip the boy up, came the great dog, Bran, his jaws wide,

his red tongue lolling. His shaggy face was ferocious—
but his eyes twinkled merrily at the two grown-ups who
stood beneath the apple-tree.

'Stand still and surrender, you Romans!' yelled Caracalla, 'If you value your lives! Down with Rome! Up
the Catuvellauni!'

Bran gave a great yelp and took the hem of Myrina's
robe in his jaws, pretending to shake it savagely.

Then Marcus Titus put his arm round Myrina and
smiled a strange smile, half-sad, half-happy, as the two
raced down the hill again, boy and dog.

'They have won another battle,' said Myrina. 'Look
how proudly Bran runs, the silly old thing! His coat
really needs shearing again, if he is to gallop about in
your sunshine like that!'

And truly, Bran had never felt prouder in his life; no,
not even when he stood by Gwyn's chariot at Camulodunum.

The Background to this Story

MANY of us have the idea that Britain was conquered by Julius Caesar, and that the 'Ancient Britons' were shaggy savages who lived in caves and used nothing better than crude stone axes. This is all wrong!

Caesar certainly *did* visit Britain, in 55 and 54 B.C., but he didn't stay very long or travel very far. One could say that his main reason for coming was not to conquer Britain, but to get to know more about our island and the various tribes which inhabited it.

The *real* invasion started in 43 A.D.—almost a hundred years later—by the order of the new Roman Emperor, Claudius, who wished to show the people at home that he was a strong ruler. More than 30,000 Romans landed near the Medway, then came north across the Thames, and so directed one of their main attacks against Colchester, which was then called Camulodunum and was the chief city of Caratacus, one of the main British 'kings.'

After Camulodunum fell, Caratacus retreated to the south-west, where there were many already ancient hill-fortresses. It is thought that he put up quite a stand in one of these, Maiden Castle, or Mai Dun, in Dorset. But eventually the Romans, now under a General named Vespasian (who later became an Emperor himself!) drove him out. The once-proud British king still fought on, in a number of places in Wales and perhaps in Shropshire; but he was beaten in the end. He made the mistake of going into what is now Yorkshire for help from the ambitious British Queen Cartimandua. She wished to gain favour with the Romans, and so gave him up, to be sent as a prisoner to Rome.

One cheering thing comes out of this: when Caratacus stood before Emperor Claudius to receive his punishment, the Roman—really a pleasant, scholarly person with many troubles of his own—so admired him that he pardoned the Briton, and even gave him a pension so that he and his family could live in comfort in Rome.

As for the 'Ancient Britons' being hairy savages—we must put that right! Certainly, there had been such people—perhaps 2,000 years earlier! But by 43 A.D. the Britons (who really should be called 'the Celts') were no more backward, say, than the Germans, or even the Gauls who lived in France, and who were very closely related to the Britons. In fact, some families had branches in both Gaul and in Britain and visited each other fairly frequently.

The most civilized 'tribes' in Britain were perhaps the Catuvellauni, Trinovantes, Iceni and Brigantes. Caratacus (and please note that this spelling is correct!) belonged to the Catuvellauni, a people who came originally from what is now Belgium. They had their own coinage, not unlike that of certain parts of Greece, and were experts in metal-work and in the use of brightly-

coloured enamels. Their fine brooches and gold bracelets would delight almost any fashion-proud lady living
today.

Of course, these Celts were fierce in battle: but, after
all, so was your father, perhaps, in the last war—especially if he was a Commando, or sailed in a battleship
or a destroyer or a submarine, or flew in Fighter or
Bomber Command. Soldiers have to be fierce, unfor-
tunately.

And, talking about soldiers, just a few words about
the Roman Legions themselves. An ordinary foot-
soldier signed-up to serve with the 'Colours', or Eagles,
for twenty years; after which he was discharged and
given land and a pension. Every ten men were under the
command of a *Decurion*, and every hundred men under
a *Centurion*. A *Tribune*, whom we would probably call
a Staff Officer, had control of a thousand soldiers; and
above him would come the Camp Prefect, and then the
Legionary Legate, or General.

There is not much more to say, without going into
detail—but the main thing to remember is that the men
and women of this story were not really very much
different from ourselves. Of course, they hadn't got
radio and plastics and breakfast cereals in cardboard
packets—but don't forget the Bible had already been
written, and so had the great plays of Sophocles and
Euripides, and also the poetry of Homer. But if this
doesn't mean much to you, just remember that geo-
metry was 350 years old when Bran, the war dog, made
his first tottering puppy-steps beside his mother,
Rhianna!

HENRY TREECE